PUBLIC AFFAIRS

A LESBIAN ANTHOLOGY

VICTORIA RUSH

COPYRIGHT

For the uninhibited...

VOLUME ONE

RUSH HOUR

1

DANGEROUS LIAISONS

I'd been looking forward to my first visit to New York City for months. After hearing so much about The Big Apple from TV shows, movies, and friends, I'd crammed a busy itinerary into my short one-week stay. Broadway, the Metropolitan Museum, Rockefeller Center, shopping on 5th Avenue—there was so much to do in so little time.

But first, there was the little matter of my three-day business conference. The largest graphic design trade show of the year was running at the Javits Center in midtown Manhattan, and it was something I felt I couldn't pass up. Besides displaying all the latest technology in the ever-changing landscape of graphic design software, all the big media companies would be there. As a freelance artist, there were simply too many potential customers to ignore.

It would have been easier to take a cab to get to my venue, but today I wanted to experience an authentic New York rite of passage by taking the subway. As I walked down the front steps of my hotel toward the 103rd Street subway station one block away, I marveled at the majestic trees lining Central Park West. The city park was definitely on my to-do list, and I planned to take a long stroll later in the day to absorb the autumn color.

When I descended the stairs to the underground concourse, I was surprised how busy the station was. There was a heavy flow of commuters streaming into the station, and the subway platform was already four or five people deep waiting for the next rush hour train to arrive. I purchased a MetroCard at one of the vending machines, then scurried through the turnstiles onto the packed platform.

Suddenly, the station filled with a deafening roar as two trains raced into the terminal from opposite ends. The southbound train screeched to a halt in front of me and opened its doors, and a small group of people shuffled off the train. Then the dense crowd on the platform converged on the narrow opening, trying to squeeze into the tight cabin. I wasn't prepared for the aggressiveness of the passengers as they pushed and jostled past me toward the door. Within ten seconds, the car was filled to capacity as a wall of passengers stood by the lip of the door, blocking the opening.

Holy crap, I thought. *My friends weren't kidding when they said everything moves faster in Manhattan.*

I stepped back from the opening and watched the passengers squeeze their shoulders together to allow enough room for the door to close.

At least next time, I breathed a sigh of relief, *I'll be at the front of the line.*

Within a minute, another train roared into the station. I quickly stepped to the side of the door nearest me and waited for the exiting passengers to leave the compartment. When I stepped into the carriage, I noticed it was already half full. The surge of passengers streaming in behind me pushed me deeper into the car and off to the side. The seats were already taken, so I found a spot in the corner beside the exit door and grabbed hold of the overhead support bar to steady myself. A pretty brunette was seated in the single chair on the end wall, reading Cosmo.

"Excuse me," I said, wiggling in next to her, trying to find a spot with a few inches of personal space.

She smiled at me and nodded, then returned her attention to her magazine. Passengers continued filtering into the subway car, pushing and squeezing us closer together. By the time the doors closed, I scarcely had an inch to breathe, and I could feel bodies pressing up against me from the sides and behind. I grasped the overhead bar more firmly and spread my feet a few inches to get a solid footing. I glanced at the people resting on the seats below me and noticed that everyone was either tapping on their cell phones or reading a newspaper.

When the train picked up speed and was swallowed in the blackness of the underground tunnel, I looked in the reflected light of the window in front of me to scan the activity in my car. Everybody seemed to be staring impassively ahead or reading the advertisements above the windows. As the train rattled through the tunnel jostling back and forth, I could feel the surrounding passengers shifting their weight against me. Someone's hips were pressing into my ass, and I looked in the window to see a pretty college-aged girl wearing a backpack with the NYU logo. The feeling of having someone touching me so intimately in the tight confines of the subway car was turning me on, and I felt my pussy beginning to tingle.

I tilted my hips toward her to try to get her attention, but she seemed lost in conversation as her fingers flicked over her cellphone screen. Glancing to my side, I noticed the seated brunette had lifted her gaze from her magazine and was watching my ass rubbing against the college girl's hips directly in front of her. She looked up in my direction, then turned to our reflected image in the window and smiled at me. I blushed at the realization that she'd caught me trying to grab a cheap feel on the subway train and quickly turned my head in the other direction. But there was something about the way she looked at me that got my juices flowing even stronger.

When the train entered the next station and our car doors opened, I was sad to see the college girl leave the compartment. A new surge of passengers boarded the cabin, then the brunette stuffed her magazine in her purse and stood up to take a position on my left side. She was so close to me, I could smell her perfume. She reached onto the support handle and grasped the bar beside my hand. The feeling of her warm skin next to mine on the cool bar sent a charge through my body.

Another passenger squeezed in behind us, taking her vacant seat on the end wall, and I glanced at the brunette in the window reflection and smiled. She was a little younger than me, maybe in her early thirties, and dressed in a tight-fitting business suit that hugged her curvy body. She had big brown eyes and sexy full lips, and I blushed when she caught me checking out her body.

We were packed like sardines in the tight confines of the subway car, and I felt the brunette's hips press against the side of my ass. I wasn't sure if she was doing it intentionally or just trying to provide some more space for the last few passengers squeezing into our end of the car. Either way, it was a pleasant feeling, and I kept my feet firmly planted and my body erect, maintaining the pressure between us.

When the train left the station and accelerated into the tunnel, the shifting weight of the carriage caused our bodies to bump together, creating a different kind of friction between us. I could feel her hard pubis pushing against my cheeks, and I squeezed my glutes to provide a firmer surface for her to get more direct stimulation. To my delight, she began moving her hips rhythmically against my ass, and I felt her wetness soaking through the thin microfiber on the back of my pants.

She was tribbing me in the tight confines of the subway car, with nobody the wiser!

I looked in the car window and gave her a knowing smile, then to remove all doubt as to whether I was a willing participant in the equation, I began moving my hips in rhythm with hers. If there was anything I could do to help her get off in the secrecy of our confined space, I was only too happy to help. The pace of her gyrations began to pick up and as her mouth parted, I could feel the coolness of her breath against my neck. She interlaced her fingers with mine on the overhead bar and squeezed my hand. As we watched each other in the reflected glass, her mouth opened wider and the look on her face contorted in sweet agony.

By now, my own pussy was flooded with lubrication, and I could feel the wetness accumulating in my panties. I was dying for some stimulation of my own, but I couldn't move my free hand in direct view of the seated passengers in front of me. Even though they seemed preoccupied with other matters, it was simply too risky. I tried to reach behind me with my right hand to touch the brunette, but she was on the wrong side. All I could do was squeeze my left butt cheek to provide a hard surface for her to rub against and provide a little extra stimulation by tilting my hips quietly in rhythm with her.

Suddenly, she stopped moving, as she pressed her pussy firmly against my backside and squeezed my hand tightly on the bar. I saw her head bob forward in a series of spastic lurches as she grimaced trying to stifle her pleasure.

I'd never seen anything so hot in my entire life. The notion of having sex on a crowded train, even between two fully-clothed people, was insanely arousing. This was my first experience with illicit public sex, and I was already addicted. Even my experiences on the Nude Cruise couldn't match this, knowing that everybody already had tacit approval to engage in public sex in the erotic-themed venues. But sex on a *train* was a definite no-no, where one or both of us could be charged with a crime, especially if it was found to be nonconsensual.

But this was definitely *consensual*. I was more than a willing partner, and I wanted *more*.

I was glad when the train roared into the next station, providing a bit of a distraction. It gave me a chance to shift position with the pretty brunette, so we could reciprocate favors. As people began to shuffle out of our car, I stepped aside to give her some space to move in front of me. This would have given me a bit more privacy and an opportunity to stimulate my own clit, but she reached out and pressed her hand gently against my back. Apparently, she had other ideas. I wasn't sure what she had in mind, and I frowned as a new round of passengers crowded into our end of the car, pressing us together in the previous position.

I looked in the window and furrowed my eyebrows at the brunette, wondering what she was thinking. She simply smiled at me and blew me a silent kiss as she pressed her hips against my pliant ass. This time, as soon as the train entered the darkened tunnel, I felt her right hand circle under my buttocks and two fingers press into the opening between my legs.

God, yes! I thought, catching my breath from her intrusion into my private zone.

I glanced at the two people seated directly in front of me to see if they'd noticed the unusual movement only two feet away from them at their same eye level. A young woman was busy texting on her phone and a businessman had his head buried in the spread of the New York Times, oblivious to what was going on around them. And the people standing beside me were either peering at the ads on the wall or reading their phones.

Thank God for smartphones.

The brunette now had a green light to pretty much do whatever she wanted with me in the tight confines of our noisy subway car. Nobody could see or hear what was going on below their line of sight. I spread my feet a few inches further apart to give her freer access to my underside, then tilted my hips back to move my throbbing clit closer to her hand. My pants were now thoroughly soaked through with my love juices, and the brunette slid her fingers through the cleft in my labia created by the tight seam of my dress pants.

How I wished I'd worn a skirt instead of pants on this first day of the conference!

But it didn't really matter since she probably could have gotten me off even if I was wearing a chastity belt, I was so worked up by now. I looked at her in the glass, and she winked at me as she rolled my erect clit between her thumb and her forefinger. I gasped out loud, then coughed a few times when some of the seated passengers looked up, trying to divert attention from what was going on. The brunette paused briefly until everybody's attention returned to their reading material.

Not knowing how much longer we'd have before being interrupted at the next stop or if someone might catch on to what we were doing, I was eager to get off as soon as possible. I parted my legs another inch and tilted my hips back as far as I could to signal that I was ready. The brunette looked at me intently in the window then she began to rub my clit more firmly. I closed my eyes and exhaled from the pleasure emanating between my legs and began to sway my hips in tandem with the movement of her fingers.

I began to hear the familiar echo sound of the train approached another station, and I squeezed my buttock muscles to speed the arrival of my orgasm. Just as the train raced into the new station, I felt the passion engulf me, and I clamped down on the brunette's fingers and bit my tongue, trying to stifle my moans. I'd never had to work so hard to conceal the powerful orgasm washing over me. The contractions seemed to go on forever, and I was worried I'd still be coming as people began to shuffle off the train.

But the timing was perfect, and the last waves of my orgasm subsided just as the train came to a stop. But by this time, I was so worried that someone might have noticed us, that I pulled away from the overhead bar and began making my way off the train. I hated to leave the brunette so abruptly, but I was too embarrassed that we'd be found out. Besides, I couldn't continue on to my business conference with this giant wet spot between my legs. I'd have to go back to my hotel for a change of clothes before going any further.

As I got off the car and headed toward the station exit to catch a cab, I paused in the middle of the platform and turned around as the train began to pull away. The brunette and I made eye contact, and we smiled at one another. We'd shared a powerful silent connection that would forever stay between the two of us.

DRESS UP

That night I could hardly sleep. I couldn't stop thinking about what had happened on the subway. I came three more times visualizing the memory of the brunette fingering me on the crowded train. It wasn't just the idea of having public sex that turned me on, it was the *danger* of the act that brought it to a new level. If either one of us had been caught, we could have been charged with indecent behavior and led out of the station in handcuffs. When I finally did nod off, I dreamt of being fondled by multiple strangers, surrounded by oblivious travelers focused on other distractions.

I woke up with a giant wet spot on the sheets and staggered to the shower to get ready in time for day two of my conference. I figured the previous day's encounter was a once-in-a-lifetime fluke, where I just happened to find myself next to someone bold enough to make a brazen public advance. But I planned to be ready just in case. I wore a loose-fitting summer dress with no bra or panties, and three-inch platform sandals to provide easier access to my undercarriage. This time, there'd be no need to rush back to my hotel to change my soiled undergarments. Even if I wasn't able to hook up with the pretty brunette again, just the sensation of feeling the swirling air from the moving train on my bare pussy would be a thrill.

I knew it was a longshot that I'd find the brunette in the same place on the same train on two consecutive days. But she looked like a regular commuter, and I figured that if I timed it right, I might get lucky. I glanced at my watch and noticed that it was 7:30. I grabbed my purse and rushed out of my hotel room, already feeling the moisture building between my legs.

When I got to the subway station, I slipped my MetroCard through the card reader then paused to get my bearings. I remembered turning to the right yesterday after passing through the turnstiles to get away from the crowd, but I couldn't recall how far down the platform I'd gone before getting on the train. Then I noticed a familiar advertisement on the side wall. I walked toward it and stepped forward to get closer to the edge of the platform. I didn't want to risk missing my train twice in as many days.

After a few minutes, a train rattled into the station, and I swiveled my head trying to catch sight of the pretty brunette in one of the passing cars. But it was moving too fast and the cars were too full to make out any familiar faces. When the train came to a halt, I scanned inside the adjacent car, but I didn't see the brunette. I hesitated, unsure whether to enter the compartment.

Had I missed her train? I thought. *Was I too early, or too late? Should I wait for the next one to see if I can find her on that one?*

I searched frantically through the window at the south end of the carriage, but it was too densely packed with passengers to make anything out. Thinking she'd taken another seat out of view, I stepped into the car just before the door closed. As the train sped out of the station, I pushed my way through the crowd toward the end wall. When I got to the far corner, I was disappointed to see no sign of the brunette. I squeezed toward the window and grabbed hold of the overhead support bar. To my surprise, the same college girl who'd been standing behind me yesterday was seated on the bench in front of me, reading a book.

I craned my head toward the other end of the cabin to look for any sign of the brunette. Just when I was beginning to despair about ever seeing her again, a familiar scent tickled my nose. *That perfume! Could it be—.* I glanced in the window reflection and saw the brunette pushing her way through the crowd in my direction.

She was a creature of habit, after all. Or maybe she just had the same idea I had—that if she got on the same train at the same time in the same place, she might be lucky enough to find that special someone who shared her predilection for public sex.

When she came up beside me, she took the position as yesterday, just to my left and behind me. Then she reached up and placed her hand over mine on the overhead bar and smiled at me in the window. She ran her eyes up and down my body, noticing my change of clothes and nodded with approval. Then she pressed in closer behind me and I felt her hand reach under my dress and squeeze my butt cheek. My ass trembled in excitement at her touch, and I spread my legs as far as I could to give her more space to reach between my legs.

She wasted no time plunging three fingers into my aching snatch, and I gasped out loud in pleasure. The college girl glanced up from her book and I coughed into my hand to distract her attention. The brunette paused until everybody's attention returned to their reading material, then she resumed finger-fucking me. I leaned over to tilt my pussy in her direction and noticed the college girl was no longer peering down at her book. Her eyelashes fluttered under her brow as she stared straight ahead at my dress. I wasn't sure if she'd noticed the brunette's hand movement under my garment, or if she merely suspected what was going on. Either way, I began to get worried and stopped moving my hips while I stared into the brunette's eyes in the window, trying to signal for her to stop before we got caught.

Fortunately, the train roared into the next station providing a temporary diversion. As it began to spit out passengers and take on a fresh load, the brunette pulled her fingers out of my pussy and began circling my clit. She was enjoying watching me squirm, and she had no intention of stopping her little tease. I closed my eyes and bit my lip as the new crop of passengers squeezed and pushed in behind us.

I noticed the college girl hadn't gotten off at the same stop as yesterday and saw that she was still peering straight ahead at my dress. I looked up at the brunette, pleading for her to stop until the train left the station. At least in the relative privacy of the darkened tunnel, the increased noise and jostling of the train would provide a temporary distraction from prying eyes. I wasn't sure if the brunette had also noticed the college girl's diverted attention. She simply smiled at me in the window as if to say: *So what if someone notices? Live in the moment, and revel in the extra attention.*

When the train finally sped out of the station, I glanced at the subway map over the window and saw that our next stop was 86th Street. We wouldn't have long to finish our business before the next interruption. Sensing my concern, the brunette thrust her thumb into my pussy and began massaging my clit with the cup of her hand. I groaned softly and twisted my face in pleasure as she watched my tortured agony in the window.

I had to fight the temptation not to rock my hips, and I pushed down on her hand so she could fuck me deeper with her thumb. I was gushing all over her, and I was worried that someone might hear the suspicious sloshing sound emanating from between my legs. But the train must have been running behind schedule, and the sound of it racing through the noisy tunnel overpowered every other sound in the compartment.

I glanced down at the college girl and saw that she'd placed her book on her lap, cradling it open with two hands under its spine. Her knees were slightly parted, and her right hand was moving slowly under the book. She was touching herself while she watched the brunette finger me under my dress!

The image of the girl rubbing herself while I was being fucked from behind sent a jolt through my body, and I felt my pleasure suddenly starting to rise. I caught sight of myself in the window and saw the look of ecstasy on my face and hoped that no one else was watching besides the brunette. My hard nipples were pressing against the loose cotton of my sundress, and if anybody had bothered to look up from their cell phones, it would have been obvious exactly what was going on below their line of sight.

I could feel my orgasm rising and I clenched my face to mask the intense sensations gripping my body. I couldn't believe I was about to come again surrounded by hundreds of oblivious passengers. Well, not *every* passenger. The college girl's lips parted and her eyelashes began to flutter as she neared the peak of her own pleasure.

Suddenly, her chest jerked in a series of small rhythmic spasms. Seeing her come as she watched the brunette fuck me from behind opened my own floodgates. A powerful orgasm engulfed my body and I clenched my ass cheeks together, clamping down over the brunette's hand between my legs. She watched my suffering in the window as my pussy squeezed her thumb in a series of violent contractions. My climax seemed to go forever and I twisted my face, trying to mask the incredible feeling of ecstasy washing over me.

The decibel level in the cabin suddenly rose again as the train entered the next station, finally giving me a chance to exhale and catch my breath. I wondered if the college girl noticed the puddle of fluid on the floor directly underneath me and between her legs. By the time the train stopped, my pussy finally finished pulsing, and the brunette began to retrieve her hand from between my thighs.

As passengers began exiting the train, I reached into my purse and handed her a handkerchief. She wiped her hand with the cloth, then placed it in her pants pocket and squeezed in front of me. I was disappointed she was wearing another pantsuit today, but I understood her intention clearly. There was no way I was going to leave her hanging for a second day in a row. I was dying to return the favor and give her a silent orgasm of her own.

But it wouldn't be quite as easy to disguise my attention, especially to the passengers seated directly in front of us on the bench. The college girl was flanked by two middle-aged businessmen reading the New York Times. If either one of them lowered their paper and looked up, they could easily detect the movement of my hand between the brunette's parted legs. The brunette must have been thinking the same thing, because she ducked under my outstretched arm and shifted over to my other side, directly in front of the college girl.

So she *had* noticed the girl's attention after all!

She reached up to grasp the overhead bar with her left hand and placed it next to mine. We'd switched positions now and I was the one who had clear access to her ass and erogenous regions with my dominant hand. When the train picked up speed and rocketed out of the station, I didn't waste any time. I didn't know what her regular stop was, but I looked up at the map and saw that the Javits Center stop was only four stops away. If I was going to get the brunette off in time not to miss the start of my conference for a second day, I had to get to work quickly.

When the train entered the tunnel, I moved my hand behind her ass and slipped my fingers into the crack between her legs. I gasped when I felt the moist opening of her bare slit. *Clever girl!* She'd opened the seam between her pant legs just enough for me to slip two fingers inside her. I glanced at her in the window and rejoiced as I thrust my middle and forefinger deep into her pussy. She closed her eyes and parted her legs as I felt her left pinky finger twitch on the bar next to mine.

From my new position two feet further to the side, I could now see the side of the college girl's face clearly. She was staring straight ahead, watching the movement of my hand between the brunette's parted legs. From her position directly in front of the brunette, she had a clear view of my fingers buried inside her pussy. She glanced out the corner of her eyes to ensure her seatmates were still distracted by their papers, then spread her legs gently apart. Her right hand then disappeared under her book, and when I glanced at the brunette in the window, I saw that her attention was also riveted on the girl.

I could feel the brunette's pussy growing wetter, and a soft moan emanated from her closed mouth. I smiled at the thought of her and the college girl sharing a moment, then I pulled my forefingers out of her pussy and inserted my pinky and ring fingers in their place. As I began to fuck her with my two little fingers, I pushed my forefingers forward until I found her hard nub pressing against her trousers. The college girl now had a commanding view of my fingers working the brunette's clit, while the rest of my hand fucked her hard from behind. I could feel the brunette's hips swaying as I pushed my fingers in and out of her, and the pace of her breathing increasing between her parted her lips.

Just when I thought I might be able to get her off before we hit the next stop, the train roared into the 72nd Street station. The businessmen on opposite sides of the college girl glanced up from their papers to check the station and I quickly retracted my fingers from the front of the brunette's pussy to ensure they wouldn't notice. As the passengers began to thin out beside us, I removed the rest of my hand, worried that someone might wonder what it was doing positioned so far under the brunette's ass.

It wasn't quite as easy to disguise our activity as it had been under my dress. I checked the subway map to see how long the distance was to our next stop at Columbus Circle. Then I looked at the brunette in the window and nodded, indicating that we'd have a little more time alone in the next tunnel. When I peered down at the college girl, I caught her glancing at me. I smiled at her, but she quickly lowered her head in embarrassment.

When the train left the 72nd Street Station, I glanced at the two businessmen to make sure the coast was clear, then I inserted my fingers back inside the brunette's slit. There was something about this combination of finger action that was getting me turned on, and I hoped the brunette was enjoying it as much as I was. As I thrust my little fingers into her pussy, my two forefingers pinched her clit under her trousers and I began to thrust them forward and backward.

The brunette's mouth parted and her eyes flitted with pleasure. Her cunt clamped over my fingers as she fucked my hand with her swaying hips. I glanced at the college girl and saw that her lips were parted as she panted softly, watching me finger the brunette just inches away from her face. I knew the brunette would want to make this last as long as possible, but as the train neared Columbus Circle, the pace of her hip movements sped up and the walls of her pussy pressed tighter around my fingers. As we swung into the station, her eyes flew open and she locked eyes on me as a flush rolled over her cheeks and she jerked her hips in a series of rhythmic spasms.

I glanced at the girl and saw her mouth wide open in a silent gag, almost like she was about to be sick. But I knew it was a different kind of sickness she was feeling, as she experienced her own private *petite mort.* Realizing I'd just made two beautiful women come together on a crowded subway train, my own pussy began pulsing in an involuntary orgasm. As our carriage rolled to a stop in the station, the brunette reached into her pocket and handed me my soiled kerchief. I held it to my nose briefly pretending to wipe my nose, then quietly cleaned my hands as I soaked up the sweet bouquet of our forbidden love.

3

———

DOWN AND DIRTY

When I got back to my hotel after the conference ended that day, I tore off my sundress and plunged my favorite vibrator deep inside my aching pussy. The events from the morning's train ride had been running through my head all day, and I was desperate for release. When I came, I screamed out loud, happy to be freed from the unnatural restraints of the crowded subway car. As much as I loved all the danger and secrecy of our illicit public liaison, it had been supremely difficult stifling the pleasure I felt surrounded by so many people.

That night, I had so many scenarios running through my head, it took me a long time to fall asleep. I knew there was a good chance I'd find the pretty brunette and the college girl on the next day's train, and my mind raced with all the ways the three of us could have fun. The lack of privacy in the subway car would still constrain our level of engagement, but with the college girl expressing renewed interest, we had a whole new world of possibilities. I dreamt of the three of us bare naked, screwing each other in full view of the gawking passengers.

Even though I'd only packed the one dress for this trip, I didn't hesitate to wear it again for the third day of my conference. I didn't care if anyone recognized that I was repeating my wardrobe choice. All I cared about was making it as easy as possible for the brunette, and hopefully also the college girl, to get as close and deep into me as possible. This time, I wasn't taking any chances missing the brunette's train. I left my hotel room early that day, planning to wait for them on the station platform. Something told me they wouldn't be playing so coy hiding from me in the train compartment today.

I got to the station ten minutes early and staked out a spot in the same location on the platform. I checked each passing train for any sign of the brunette, and just as I anticipated, she was standing near the window when the 7:45 rolled in. She waved at me to get my attention, and I squeezed into the compartment and pushed my way through the crowd toward the far end. When I got to the corner, the college girl was sitting in her same seat in the middle of the bench, with the brunette standing directly in front of her grasping the overhead bar with two hands.

I squeezed in next to the brunette and smiled at her in the glass, then looked down at the college girl. She was still playing hard-to-get, averting eye contact with us, but I noticed that today she was wearing a knee-length skirt instead of jeans. I was disappointed to see the brunette still hadn't gotten with the program, wearing yet another business pantsuit. I shook my head and pinched my eyebrows in the window reflection to express my dismay, but she simply nodded and smiled back at me. The look on her face was different today, like she knew something I didn't.

I glanced down at the bench again to scope out the gallery and noticed the girl was flanked today by two other girls about her same age. I didn't see any NYU logos on their paraphernalia, but they both had backpacks resting on their knees. I wasn't sure what to make of the arrangement, then I noticed they were all tapping on their phones and giggling.

This complicates the picture, I thought.

The newspapers the businessmen were reading yesterday had provided some extra cover for our dangerous liaison, but now the entire bench had a clear view directly ahead of them. I glanced up at the brunette and directed my eyes in the girls' direction to indicate my concern, but she shook her head and mouthed the words 'don't worry' to me. It was almost as if she had planned for this scenario, and she didn't seem the least bit flustered.

When the doors closed and the train accelerated out of the station, the brunette immediately took a step back and pressed her hips into my ass. My eyes flung open as I looked at her in the window. There was a hard object in her pants that felt suspiciously like a cock. I knew she wasn't transgender—I'd already felt all of her lady parts close up the previous day. Was it a vibrator, a cucumber, or some other kind of sex toy? Whatever it was, I was instantly turned on by the thought of being penetrated by her. This upped the danger quotient considerably, and my pussy was already watering in anticipation.

She unbuttoned her suit jacket and I saw her reach between her legs to make an adjustment. The girls on the bench in front of me widened their eyes, and I wondered if they could see the object between the brunette's legs. The brunette raised my dress a few inches then I felt a hard piece of rubber slap up against my vulva. I drew in a gasp of air, instantly recognizing the familiar shape. But this was no ordinary dildo, because both of the brunette's hands were otherwise occupied. Her left hand grasped the overhead bar next to mine and her right hand was resting on my hip.

What the fuck? I thought, my forehead wrinkling in confusion.

Then the brunette began to move her hips and removed all doubt.

It was a strap-on dildo! Holy shit—she planned to fuck me straight up under my dress in plain view of all the other passengers!

She tilted her hips upward trying to angle the tip of the dildo into my pussy, but she didn't have enough leverage to slip it in. She looked at me in the window and nodded, asking for an assist. I glanced at the other passengers seated on the bench in front of me and saw they were all busy tapping on their phones. I reached under the front of my dress pretending to scratch my leg and pushed the tip into my opening. The brunette took care of the rest, angling her hips and pressing forward.

The six-inch dildo quickly filled my pussy, and my eyelids flitted closed as I grunted in pleasure. The girls in front of me couldn't have seen the dildo entering me under my dress, but the action of the brunette's hips made it crystal clear exactly what was going on. The motion of her hips was unmistakable. This time she wasn't just rubbing her mound against the back of my ass, this was her full-on fucking me with a strap-on dildo!

The feeling of the hard rubber cock inside me was sublime. This was the one thing I'd missed on our previous days' trysts, and I rocked my hips gently to meet the brunette's thrusts. My lubrication was already soaking the phallus, and I could hear the faint sloshing sound it made every time the brunette rammed it into me. Some of the other passengers on the bench looked up and twisted their heads trying to detect where the sound was coming from, and the brunette slowed her pace until they looked back down at their phones.

I could feel the cock pushing and pulling my labia as it stretched the hood of my clitoris over my erect nub. The NYU girl kept looking up from her phone then back down again to type on her screen. Whether her hands were too busy texting to touch herself, or she was too engrossed in the obvious online chat she was having with her friends, was unclear. But either way, it added to the sexual tension. Although she wasn't stimulating herself like she was yesterday, I now had four voyeurs watching me instead of two.

Just as I began to feel the pleasure intensity rising in my womb, the train roared into the 96th Street station. The brunette paused again as the passengers thinned out around us and began exiting the cabin. But the feeling of having her hot poker inside me while everybody went about their everyday business was surreal, and my pussy pulsed in excitement. I was glad when a new round of passengers crowded into the compartment that nobody got up to leave the bench in front of me. I'd have the same group of distracted travelers for at least one more stop.

When the train left the station, I squeezed the brunette's hand on the overhead rail to signal I was ready for her to get me off. She nodded, then looked down at the texting girls as she slammed her rubber cock deep into my pussy. I staggered forward, almost falling on top of the passengers, and apologized for the movement of the train shifting me off balance. The three girls looked up at me and smiled slyly, knowing what had happened.

I was standing directly over them now and could see their phone screens clearly. As the brunette began to pick up her pace and slap the dildo in and out of me, I caught snippets of their online conversation.

Fuck that's hot! the NYU girl typed.

Can u believe this is happening right in front of us? one of the other girls replied.

Do u think anyone else besides us is noticing? the other one said.

Not that I can tell, the NYU girl replied, then she paused for a moment. *Are you guys getting as turned on as I am?*

Fuck, yes! her friend replied. *I want that thing inside me too!*

I'm gonna cum just watching these two, the other one said.

Knowing the girls were getting just as worked up as I was from our clandestine encounter made me even more aroused than before. I knew it wouldn't be long now before I came, and I peered at the brunette in the window to signal I was close. She removed her other hand from the overhead rail and placed it on the other side of my hips, then she pulled me toward her with her two hands and rammed the dildo even deeper into me. It had a slight downward curve, and it rubbed against my G-spot whenever she retracted it.

I could hear the echo in the distance from the approaching next station, but it didn't matter. My vagina was already tenting in preparation for a powerful orgasm, and I prepared myself for the impending climax. I spread my legs wider on the floor of the car and grasped the overhead bar with two hands. I could no longer keep my mouth closed as I panted with increasing urgency directly over the NYU girl's head, blowing her stray hairs to the side.

OMG, I'm gonna cum! she typed on her screen, as she squirmed on her seat.

That was enough for me, and I groaned as the first waves of my orgasm rolled over me. I clenched the rubber dildo and squeezed it as hard as I could as the walls of my love box spasmed in pleasure. I was glad my face was angled down over the girls' heads because it would have been impossible to mask the obvious pleasure I was experiencing to anyone else who might be watching. As my hips convulsed in uncontrolled spasms, the NYU girl's stomach tightened and she let out a tiny squeak.

At that moment, the train roared into the 86 Street station, and I felt a whoosh of fresh air rush into the cabin from a crack in the window. The sensation of the train filling the station echoed the feeling I was having from the rubber cock embedded in my pussy, and I grasped the overhead bar tightly as the NYU girl and I watched each other come, until we were thoroughly spent.

4

———

MÉNAGE À TROIS

As I stood over the college girls trying to catch my breath, I noticed the NYU girl's screen suddenly light up with new messages.

I can't wait to get off this train, one of the girls texted. *I need to touch myself right NOW!*

That's the hottest sex I've ever seen, the other one said.

What did I tell you guys? the NYU girl replied. *These are two hot mamas!*

When the train screeched to a halt, the brunette retracted the rubber dildo from between my legs, then calmly lifted it under her jacket and fastened the button. As the train began to take on a new round of passengers, the NYU girl typed a new message.

I'm going to try something, she said. *Will you guys squeeze together and take my seat?*

What are you planning to do? one of her friends replied.

You'll see.

Suddenly, the NYU girl stood up directly in front of me and turned around to face the bench, placing her hand on the bar next to mine. She caressed my hand with her forefinger then looked me straight in the eyes in the window. Apparently, this college girl wasn't as shy as I thought. I glanced at the brunette in the mirror and we nodded, recognizing what she wanted. I stepped in front of her and the brunette moved behind her, sandwiching the NYU girl between us. Her two girlfriends stopped texting on their phones and looked up at the three of us, wondering what we had planned.

When the train left the station, the brunette and I pressed our bodies tightly together, then I saw her unclasp her jacket and fumble between her legs to free the rubber dildo. She lifted one side of the girl's skirt then tilted her hips upward just as she'd done with me. I saw the girl's eyes widen in the window reflection as she felt the cock suddenly flap between her legs. But in her sandwiched position, it wasn't as easy for her to reach between her thighs to help point it where it belonged.

I moved my hand around the side of my hips and reached under the front of her skirt. The girls in front of me sat ram-straight in their seats, watching in disbelief. Just as I'd hoped, the NYU girl was bare and nude under her clothes. The feeling of her wet vulva pulsing over top of the hard dildo made my own pussy throb again. I placed my fingers under the dildo and pressed it against the girl's slit, while the brunette slid it forward and back across her opening. I could feel the girl's breath on my neck as she panted from the friction of the hard phallus against her engorged clit.

The brunette and I teased the girl for a few moments, then I pressed the tip of the dildo into her pussy with my two fingers. The girl's hips tilted away from me as she pointed her hole toward the cock. When it entered her, she moaned in my ear and kissed my neck softly. I could feel the moisture returning to my own cunt and I suddenly wished I was the one getting fucked again.

I kept my hand between the girl's legs as I felt the slippery dildo sliding in and out of her. I glanced up in the window and both the brunette and I watched the girl's face twisting in pleasure. I moved my fingers to the front of her mound and located her clit and began rubbing it in circles while the brunette pushed harder against her hips. I could see the pleasure rising on the girl's face, but we only had a short interval before the next stop at 72nd Street, and we had to pause again while everybody got off the train so as not to attract too much attention.

While the brunette kept her hips locked against the girl's ass with the dildo buried inside her, I moved my hand from under the girl's skirt and placed my wet fingers on top of hers on the overhead bar. One of her friends on the bench looked up at the NYC girl and mouthed the letters 'O - M – G' to her with wide eyes. 'So hot!' she mouthed, shifting her weight uncomfortably on her seat.

The NYU girl simply gritted her teeth and looked straight ahead, not wanting to draw any extra attention to her prostrated position. I glanced at the map on the wall and saw that our next stop was Columbus Circle. We'd have a slightly longer run before our next interruption, and I nodded to the brunette in the window that this was our chance to get the girl off.

After a new crop of passengers crowded into the compartment and the train raced back into the tunnel, I reached around behind me again and grasped the rubber joystick in my hand. The size and texture of the dildo made it almost feel like a real cock, and the girl's lubrication coating the surface made it slide effortlessly in my hand. I paused for a few moments to savor the brunette's fucking action, then I returned my fingers to the girl's love button.

She had a gloriously smooth and soft pubis, and her clit was poking out of her hood like a hot chili pepper. I pinched the tip of it between my thumb and forefinger and rolled it around. The girl whimpered in my ear as she pressed her tits into my back, resting herself against me. I pushed back with my arm on the overhead rail to support us as I began to circle her clit with my fingers.

I could feel her breath coming in stronger bursts now against the back of my neck. It was exhilarating to have such a direct connection with what she was feeling. I looked in the window and saw that she was peering directly at me now, as her eyelids fluttered in waves of pleasure. The brunette sensed she was close also, and grasped the girl's hips, thrusting the dildo deeper inside. I pressed my fingers harder against her clit and began to circle it more quickly.

The girl pressed her mouth against the top of my shoulder to stifle her moans and I saw her face tighten with her impending orgasm. Suddenly, she bit into the flesh of my shoulder and I felt her hips convulse in paroxysms of pleasure. Little squeals emanated from her mouth as she panted hot breaths on my neck as her orgasm washed over her. I held my hand over her throbbing clit while her hips jerked with each orgasmic convulsion. When she finally stopped moving, the brunette and I held the girl close, savoring the three-way connection we'd just shared. I peered down at the two other girls on the bench and they simply looked up at us with their mouths agape. We'd given them a show they would never forget.

As the train roared into Columbus Circle station, I turned around to face the girl and kissed her on her lips. The brunette withdrew the dildo from the girl's pussy and tucked it into her jacket, then she joined us in a three-way passionate kiss. We no longer cared if anyone was watching. We'd shared our own private moment of rapture, and for now at least, we were alone on our little island of ecstasy.

5

———

TUNNEL VISION

After my conference ended that day, I decided to take the next two days off to explore the city. After three escalating encounters on the subway, I felt I'd exhausted all the possibilities for illicit public sex. Besides, I knew I was pushing my chances at getting caught. The widening circle of actors in our dangerous game had reached the breaking point. It was only a matter of time before someone called us out and I'd be publicly humiliated or hauled off to jail.

But I couldn't get the thought of our clandestine trysts out of my mind. Like any dangerous habit, the more you get away with it, the greater you want to stretch the limits, and the more intoxicating it becomes. I'd sampled the poison too many times, and I needed another fix. By Saturday, it was all I could think about, and I knew I had to go back on the train one last time before leaving the city.

I figured weekend traffic would be lighter than during rush-hour, but this posed both a challenge and an opportunity. On the one hand, there'd be far fewer prying eyes, and I might even be able to find a semi-private enclave on the train to take the affair to the next level. But we also wouldn't have the advantage of being tightly packed together, where we could get away with groping each other below everyone's line of sight. Plus, there was a good chance that neither the brunette nor the college girl would be using the train on the weekend.

But it didn't matter to me. I just wanted to get back on the train and relive the memory. If I found another willing partner and the opportunity presented itself, that would be a bonus. I put my sundress on one last time and strapped on some flat sandals. There'd be no need to elevate myself to gain easier access to my undercarriage if I'd no longer be standing in a crowded car. Otherwise, I was completely bare of any accessories. The idea of being naked again under my loose dress in a public place was a thrill all in itself.

After a hearty brunch at the hotel, I headed back to the 103rd Street station. When I got to the underground concourse, I was surprised how quiet it was at mid-morning. Unlike the previous days' rush hour, there were no lineups going into the turnstiles and the subway platform was almost empty. I walked to my usual spot on the platform and noticed a handsome young man tapping on his phone.

He looked up and appraised my tanned body in my sundress and smiled at me. He was wearing loose-fitting cargo shorts and a T-shirt with sandals. I could see his muscles rippling in his powerful arms as he turned toward me, and I paused to soak up his athletic figure when he returned his attention to his phone. He had long hair dangling past a small ring in his left ear to a chiseled jaw, like some kind of hipster Adonis. When he caught me checking out his tight ass, I blushed. I was glad when the train finally rolled into the station, providing a temporary distraction.

As I expected, the carriage was almost empty. A few scattered passengers sat on the open benches and one or two people stood impassively holding the vertical support bars. There was no sign of the brunette or college girl, so I took a seat on an open bench beside the door directly opposite the young man from the platform. When the train closed its doors and sped out of the station, I crossed my legs and appraised the hipster more carefully.

He had dark eyes, a long straight nose, and carved cheeks that accentuated his Abercrombie & Fitch youthful good looks. He couldn't have been much more than twenty, and as he sat on the bench tapping his phone, he reminded me of the pretty college girl from earlier in the week. His legs were slightly parted, and I stared up his thighs, trying to steal a glance under his shorts to see if I could catch any sign of his man junk.

But he seemed lost in his phone, and I began tapping my foot impatiently to gain his attention. He looked up briefly and caught me checking him out again, but this time we lingered with a long mutual stare. He ran his eyes down my body and I lifted my leg, parting my knees slightly. Now *he* was the one staring between my legs trying to steal a glance at my private parts.

I glanced around the cabin to scope the scene and noticed a middle-aged woman reading a book on the opposing bench on the other side of the door. Another twenty-something girl had her elbows swung around a support bar tapping on her phone, waiting for her next stop. Otherwise, the Adonis and I had the entire end quarter of the carriage to ourselves. But when I looked back toward him, his head was once again buried in his phone.

I raised my left leg and placed my sandal on the bench beside me, splaying my legs in an open scissor position. My dress billowed open and I rested my hand in my lap to cover my exposed pussy. The young man looked up at the movement in his periphery, then did a double take. I smiled at him, and he shifted uncomfortably on his bench. He looked at my bare legs and ran his gaze up my body, then paused at my bosom. My nipples were growing hard from his renewed attention, and I lifted my chest to press my breasts against the loose fabric of my dress.

When he looked me straight in my eyes, I knew his phone would no longer be a distraction. I glanced at his shorts and saw one side of his pant legs tenting inward. I was obviously getting him worked up, and I was enjoying my little tease. I looked at the woman across the aisle to make sure no one else was watching, then I hiked up the left side of my dress over my knee to show the young man my bare pussy.

Suddenly, the left side of his shorts began to push outwards as I saw his penis elongate along the side of his leg. He wasn't wearing any underwear either! I couldn't believe how long his organ was as it continued to creep down the side of his pant leg. By the time it stopped growing, it had to be at least ten inches in length and two inches thick. My pussy twitched involuntarily, as I imagined what it would feel like to have him buried inside me.

Like the brunette had with her pantsuit, I'd made some adjustments to my sundress, and I slipped my right hand through a narrow opening I'd cut in the side. When the young man saw my hand emerge between my legs and begin playing with my cunny, he sat up awkwardly, trying to free his painfully constricted hard-on. The head of his cock poked out the end of his pant leg, and I began to circle my clit as I licked the top of my lip teasingly.

He glanced to his side to make sure no one else was watching, then he shimmied closer to the dividing wall beside the door and grasped the tip of his cock. He tried to rub the head awkwardly with the ends of his fingers and rocked his hips forward, trying to provide some extra friction. I spread my legs further apart to give him a better view, then moved my left hand through the slit in the other side of my dress and thrust my fingers into my open snatch.

My juices were flowing freely by now, and my hand made a nasty sucking sound as it pounded in and out of my pussy. Fortunately, the noise in the cabin from the train moving through the tunnel masked the sound for anyone further than a few feet away. The Adonis suddenly hiked up the side of his shorts and I gasped when I saw the size of his organ. Even half-unsheathed, it was longer than most other men's full-length penises.

But just as he wrapped his fist around the shaft, the train rattled into the next train station. When it stopped at the platform and new passengers began entering the compartment, he pulled his pant leg down to cover up his erection and I returned my elevated foot to the floor. An older gentleman entered the door on our end of the cabin and turned to take a seat in the far corner bench, facing me at a ninety-degree angle. The young man looked at me and frowned, knowing that our fun would be interrupted at least for a few more stops.

But my hands were still in the pockets of my dress, and I spread my legs just far enough apart for him to see my bare pussy, then I resumed touching myself. He squirmed and shuffled in his seat as he watched me finger my wet honeypot, while the old man stared straight ahead, unaware what was going on directly in front of him. I could see the young man's cock pressing against his pant leg as he rubbed it slowly under the coarse fabric of his shorts.

I felt sorry that he wasn't able to stimulate himself more directly, but he was in full view of the old man and there wasn't much he could do. I decided to have a little fun with him, and pulled my fingers out of my box then placed my hands on either side of my labia and pulled them apart. I used my pubococcyx muscles to flex the slit, teasing him to put his cock inside me. He groaned and lurched forward, trying to take some pressure off his trapped hard-on. I continued tormenting him for the next two stations, playing with myself as he looked on helplessly.

When we got to the 72nd Street stop, some more people filtered into our compartment. When two new passengers sat down on the other end of each of our benches, we both crossed our legs in frustration.

But I knew we had a longer interval before our next stop at Columbus Circle. I turned my head to look through the window into the next car and saw that it was just as busy as ours. Just then, a young teenager walked down the middle of our compartment, then opened the end door beside us and continued into the next car. I glanced at the man sitting across from me, then peered out the corner of my eyes toward the end door and back to him. He looked at me quizzically for a moment, then nodded when he understood what I was thinking.

I got up from my seat and walked to the end door and slowly lifted the latch. The sound of the noisy train barreling through the tunnel startled me, and I hesitated for a moment wondering if this was a good idea. There were no handrails to hold onto for support, only a flimsy chain flanking the gangway on both sides. I stepped through the door and turned around holding the handle for support, then closed it behind me. I was all alone now in the thundering tunnel, and the two cars pistoned back and forth as the train barreled through the dark corridor.

I looked through the glass wondering what was keeping the young man from joining me, then I saw him get out of his seat and walk toward the door. He turned the latch and stepped into the portal then closed the door behind him. We bent our knees together, trying to steady our balance over the shifting platform. I grabbed his shirt for support and looked down at the fluttering tracks racing underneath us, then I nodded to indicate we had to work quickly.

I looked through the window behind him to see if anyone was watching and was glad that everybody had redirected their attention, assuming we had passed through like the teenager. Then I turned around and placed my hands on the wall of the next car and lifted my dress over my ass. The young man got the message and unzipped his shorts then braced his feet on the narrow platform and pushed his hips forward. I felt his python slap up against the underside of my pussy, and I tilted my hips to give him freer access.

Unlike with the brunette's strap-on dildo, he didn't need a helping hand getting inside me. His springy cock quickly angled up toward my opening and I could feel the slippery head push my lips apart as he entered me. Bombarded with all the sensations from the train rocketing through the tunnel, it was the most intense feeling I'd ever felt. From the smell of the burning steel in the tunnel, to the roar of the train racing through the corridor, to the feeling of cool air rushing between my legs as the man thrust his giant cock into my pussy—I was stimulated to the maximum degree possible, in every imaginable way.

As the Adonis pounded his manhood into me, I struggled to maintain my balance on the shifting platform. I was suddenly glad we had a limited time to finish our business, and I began rocking my hips in concert with his thrusts to bring us both to completion. The young man reached through the hole in one side of my dress and lifted it higher as he cupped and pinched my breasts. If anybody was looking through the glass at the end of the compartment, they were certainly getting a hell of a show.

The Adonis began thrusting his cock with more urgency, and I could feel my own passion beginning to rise. This sex-on-a-train idea was *insane*, but I was loving every minute of it. Beyond the danger of someone reporting us, there was the distinct possibility either one of us could fall to our deaths on the tracks below at any moment.

I grasped the handle of the door in front of me and pressed my face against the glass as the man pushed and lifted me forward. I screamed in pleasure, and I saw a few people turn from inside the compartment to look in my direction. With the familiar sound of the approaching station filling the tunnel, the man pushed his other hand under my dress and grasped me hard by the side of my hips.

I could feel his cock flaring inside me and I knew he was close. With one final thrust, he pressed his pelvis hard against my ass and held me tight while I gushed all over his glorious firehose. While we glued ourselves together in spastic union, I watched the passengers standing on the adjacent platform race by the narrow opening between our two cars as the train poured into Columbus Circle station. When it finally came to a stop, the young man pulled his dripping penis out of me, zipped up his shorts, and the two of us walked nonchalantly into the next cabin, as the stunned passengers watched us exit the train.

Being caught red-handed having sex on the subway was more fun than I thought it would be.

VOLUME TWO

NUDE CRUISE

EXOTIC VOYAGE

My exhilarating encounters at the dinner party, the dark room, and naked yoga had whet my appetite for new adventures. But each of these experiences, as stimulating and fulfilling as they were in their own right, were one-time affairs. In each case, it hadn't taken long for me to yearn for something new, something more. I wanted an *all-in-one* adventure, where I could move from one new experience to another without having to search for the next one. I wanted my own erotic *Disneyland*.

I knew if I could find such diverse activities online, there must be a whole underworld of swingers looking for something similar. Surely some enterprising operator would see the potential in putting together some kind of package deal. I sat down in front of my computer, opened up my browser, and typed in the words 'all-inclusive erotic adventure.'

A surprising number of 'clothing-optional' resort listings came up. I clicked on the first one, but it just showed the usual pictures of pretty pools, beaches, and guests suites, with a vague description of an 'upscale retreat for an adventurous lifestyle experience'. A little further down the page, I saw a blog article titled *Inside a nudist sex resort*. The article described an adventure traveler's experience at a resort where couples romped on nude beaches, swam in nude pools, and 'hooked up' in private cabins.

Definitely a little too tame-sounding for me.

I clicked on the next page of search results, where I saw a link titled *Nude Cruise — Explore Your Erotic Fantasies.*

This looks interesting.

I clicked on the link and a webpage opened showing pictures of naked people climbing walls, dancing in water fountains, and wrestling in a muddy pit.

That looks a little different, I thought.

At the top of the webpage, there was a tab titled *Fantasy Menu.* I clicked on the link, and a list of sexy-sounding shipboard activities appeared:

> Peak Sensation
> House of Holes
> Fantasy Fountain
> Sensuous Steam Room
> Masquerade Ball
> Sexy Games Room
> Get Down Disco
> Cybersex Rules
> Private View Rooms
> Intimate Massage
> FourPlay

I clicked on the first one and a photo appeared showing naked men and women scaling a climbing wall with unusual foot and hand holds. Instead of the usual jug and pocket holds, the 'grips' were in the shape of dildos and artificial vaginas, where climbers could pause to 'rest' and 'recharge their batteries' as they scaled the wall. A description under the photo read:

Challenge yourself to a climbing wall like no other. The higher you go, the more stimulating the experience becomes. Reward yourself at each new level, where you'll find a new wall feature to stimulate and excite every part of your body, as you seek the peak experience at the top of the mountain. All while safely strapped into a comfortable harness that permits a maximum range of movement and accessibility.

That sounds like an incredible turn on, I thought.

The idea of fucking a dildo strapped to a wall while people watched me from below sounded insanely sexy. My pussy began to twitch as I imagined the idea.

What's this next one—*House of Holes*?

I clicked on the next listed activity, and a picture appeared showing various nude men and women pressing their hips and buttocks against a wall with scattered holes. The look of ecstasy on their faces left little doubt as to what was happening on the other side. The description read:

Hook up with a stranger on the other side of a wall through your own personal intimate portal. You can choose to 'give', 'receive', or 'merge' with a partner of either sex in an erotic and completely anonymous connection. Or you can choose to simply watch, as other couples get their groove on in this sensuous and erotic House of Holes.

Damn, that sounds dirty. And fun.

I'd heard of glory holes before, but I'd always thought of them as skanky places where gay men went to get an anonymous blow job. The idea of engaging in heterosexual sex or touching pussies with another woman through my own private portal was different. And highly stimulating. My left hand dropped down between my legs and I began to rub my clit as I continued exploring the website.

What happens in the Sexy Games Room?

I clicked on the next activity, which displayed a photo of naked men and women in contorted positions atop a polka-dot-covered mat. Their hips and asses were pressed together while they stretched their arms and legs around each other. The caption read:

Play interactive nude games with your fellow guests where the rules and rewards are wide open. With Naked Twister, stretch into increasingly difficult and erotic positions as you try to reach around, over, and under your naked partners. Or try Naked Poker where the 'loser' must engage in increasingly erotic situations in full view of their playing partners. Or jump into the Naked Mud Wrestling pit and try to wrestle your partner into submission, all while surrounded in sensuous mud.

Fuck, yes! I thought. *These guys know how to organize an erotic party.*

I didn't need to click any more of the fantasy activities to know this was the sort of erotic travel destination that I had in mind. It promised to be an immersive, stimulating experience with multiple partners and exciting activities. As always though, I needed to be sure it would be clean and safe. I searched the page and found a tab marked *Conditions*, which read:

Every Nude Cruise guest must provide a certified report from a verified medical testing lab, indicating negative for sexually communicated diseases. The report must be dated within one week of your ship's departure date. Clothing is optional for all activities. Security staff are available at all venues to ensure the safety of guests and to ensure that all interaction occurs only with express consent.

Fair enough, I thought. *The medical test requirement shows this is a class act. You can't be too careful about these things.*

I clicked the Booking tab and viewed the calendar for available dates. The next cruise departed from Miami in two weeks' time. I'd have to move a few things around and schedule a two-hour flight, but one of the joys of my job as a freelance graphic designer meant I could choose my own vacation days. I booked a private cabin with a Queen-size bed, then I tore my panties off and plunged my fingers into my pussy as I fantasized about all the shipboard activities I'd soon be participating in.

2

SETTING SAIL

On the scheduled day of my departure, my whole body was buzzing with excitement. This was my first cruise, and I didn't know what to expect. Besides my fear of seasickness, I was a little nervous about the idea of parading around nude in public. I'd picked up some anti-nausea pills at the pharmacy, but I had butterflies in my stomach for an entirely different reason.

So far, my excursions into the realm of public sex and nudity had been fairly anonymous. At the dinner party, I could hide behind my masquerade mask. In the dark room, the special light effects concealed my identity. Even at my naked yoga class, everybody was so busy concentrating on their poses that it was really only my partner who had a close-up view of me.

But on this 'clothing-optional' cruise, I'd be going about my everyday routines in plain view of hundreds of strangers. Granted, some of the activities sounded highly erotic and fun. But the idea of sitting down for dinner or even just sunbathing in the nude gave me the willies. I'd packed some skimpy bikinis in case I got cold feet, but I didn't want to be the only one wearing clothes if everyone else was naked.

When I arrived at the cruise terminal, it was a hive of activity.

There were hundreds of people waiting to go through security, and the building was buzzing with chatter and public announcements. I pulled out my boarding pass and looked for the sign directing me to my designated gate. Just like at airport security, there were multiple lines of people placing their bags on conveyor belts going through an X-ray machine. When it was my turn, I took off my shoes and opened my roller-bag to remove my liquids.

"That won't be necessary, ma'am," a handsome security attendant said.

"Oh?" I murmured, confused.

"No need to remove your shoes or any items from your bag," he said. "Security procedures for cruise ships aren't as stringent as they are for air travel."

I smiled and nodded sheepishly as I pulled my sandals back on.

"Unless you're carrying something metal, of course. That'll set our machine off."

"No, of course not," I said, blushing from all the attention I was getting holding up the line. But now I was worried about the vibrator I'd packed in my luggage.

Who needs to bring a vibrator on a naked sex cruise, anyway? I chided myself.

"I'll just need to see your boarding pass," the security agent said.

I showed him my pass, and he directed me to stand in line behind the pass-through body scanner. As I waited for my turn, I looked around at my fellow boarding passengers. Most of them were fairly young, in their 20s and 30s, but there were also some older couples who were apparently looking for a little adventure to spice up their marriages. I noticed a few people checking each other out. Most of them didn't make eye contact for very long, but I wasn't the only one undressing some of the hot passengers with my eyes.

I caught a tanned gentleman in the adjacent line running his eyes up and down my body. I'd intentionally worn skinny jeans and a tight blouse for the first day to show off my best assets. I stood up tall and lifted my chest to display my cleavage. He had a nice ass, strong arms, and beautiful skin. When our eyes met, he smiled at me, and I could feel the blood rushing to my face again.

Come on, Jade, I admonished myself. *Get a hold of yourself. If you're going to be this self-conscious fully clothed, how are you ever going to be comfortable walking around in the nude?*

I returned my attention to the X-ray machine as my bag disappeared under the cover. I watched the face of the security agent as he scanned the monitor for any suspicious contents, then breathed a sigh of relief when I saw my bag pop out the other end.

"Ma'am?" the agent at the opposite side of the body scanner said, motioning for me to step through.

I'd been so worried my vibrator would set off the X-ray machine, that I hadn't realized I was holding up the line again. I nodded self-consciously, then walked through the pass-through stand, making eye contact with the security agent to ensure I wouldn't set off any other alarms. After he nodded that I was clear, I picked my bag off the X-ray belt and looked for the sign to the check-in area. By now, I was sure that half the passengers in the security area were cursing in bewilderment at my awkward travel etiquette, and I was glad to find a respite at the end of a new line.

"That's a pretty big bag for a short cruise," a woman's voice said, as I heard someone step up behind me.

I turned around and looked into the eyes of a stunning brunette about my same height.

"Um, well, you know," I stammered. "It's mostly makeup and toiletries and that sort of thing. We women can't be shorthanded about these things."

I could feel the flush in my cheeks again, caught off guard by her disarming beauty.

"No, I suppose not," she said, smiling at my innocence. "Although something tells me *makeup* will be the least of our concerns on this trip."

Her confidence and bold manner was rapidly sending blood flowing to another part of my body.

"Is this your first time with this cruise operator?" I asked, not wanting to state the obvious.

"This is my third Fantasy Cruise. Once you dip your toes in, it's kind of addicting." Her eyes darted across my face, appraising my demeanor. "How about you?"

"It's my first time. I'm a bit nervous, to be honest. You know, about all the..."

"Yeah, there's a lot of that," she said. "But there's nothing to worry about. We're all in the same boat, so to speak. You get used to it pretty fast. It's actually quite liberating. Not having to dress up and put on airs. Nudity is a great equalizer."

I took a quick glance at her tight and tanned body. She was wearing loose fitting linen shorts and a tight T-shirt displaying a cruise ship sailing into the sunset. Her legs were long and shapely, and her firm breasts sat up high on her chest.

"Some of us are a little more equal than others, I'm afraid."

She scanned my figure and smiled.

"I don't think you have anything to worry about. You're gorgeous. As long as you don't mind being the center of attention with a body like that."

I puffed out my cheeks and exhaled heavily.

"That's exactly what I'm worried about. I'm not used to being the center of attention. At least not in a public setting with all my clothes off."

"What deck is your cabin on?" she asked.

I fumbled for my travel papers and pulled out my boarding pass.

"E deck," I said. "They told me that if I chose a cabin nearer the water line, I have a better chance of avoiding seasickness."

"That's my deck too. Stick with me girl, and I'll show you around. There are plenty of ways to take your mind off the motion of the boat. The key is to not stay in one place too long. With so many interesting shipboard activities, your stomach will be the *last* thing you'll be thinking about."

She held out her hand and smiled at me.

"My name's Heather."

"Jade," I said, shaking her hand softly. "Thanks, Heather. I could use a wing woman, or shipmate, or whatever you're supposed to call your cruise partner these days."

"It's a deal," Heather said, winking at me. "We'll be *partners in crime*."

I reached the front of the line and saw one of the check-in agents motioning for me to come to her station.

"I'll wait for you past check-in," I said, suddenly mindful of the increasing dampness building between my legs.

3

RECEPTION

After clearing through Check-in, Heather guided me through the final boarding process then we walked together toward our rooms on E deck. We agreed to meet thirty minutes later when we'd go to the guest reception in the main lounge on the top deck. Our rooms were in the same hall, so after saying temporary goodbyes, I continued down the hall toward my stateroom.

When I opened my door, I was surprised by how small my room was. The Queen-size bed seemed to take up almost all of the space, with a tiny adjoining closet and small desk beside the wall-mounted TV. I went into the bathroom and was disappointed to see a stand-up shower with no tub. I knew that space aboard a cruise ship was at a premium, but I wasn't expecting it to feel so claustrophobic.

I unpacked my toiletries and placed them on the tiny sink, then carried my small carry-on case and placed it on the bed. There was a small sliding window beside my bed, and I immediately walked over and slid it open to breathe in some fresh air. I could see a flotilla of small boats moving about the bay opposite our ship, and I immediately regretted not upgrading to a larger room with balcony.

I bet Heather has a bigger room, I thought. *I'm such a lightweight at this cruise thing.*

I was looking forward to picking her brain for other tips about optimizing my shipboard experience. Not to mention picking over the *rest* of her body. I couldn't wait to see her naked and run my hands over her tight ass and breasts.

The porter had taken my larger roller case, and I didn't have much of a change of clothes in my carry-on bag. Heather had said not to worry too much about what to wear for the reception since most first-time guests chose not to go fully nude at the first activity. Nevertheless, I wanted to get with the program and ease myself into the idea of being naked on board, so I removed my bra and unbuttoned my silk blouse three buttons to reveal my cleavage.

I went into the washroom and looked at myself in the small mirror. The soft silk rubbing against my nipples had already stimulated them to an aroused state, and they protruded against the thin fabric, creating two conspicuous nodes. I smiled at how full and firm my breasts looked in my revealing blouse and hoped they'd attract Heather's attention too. I put on a new coat of light red lipstick and touched up my mascara, then grabbed my purse and headed down the hall toward Heather's room.

When she opened her door and I saw what she was wearing, it took my breath away. She wore a see-through gauzy top that barely concealed her large breasts through the sheer material. I stared shamelessly at her figure, wanting to flip her loose top up over her waist and devour her firm, round tits. To top it off, she'd let her long brown hair down and it shone with iridescent hues of amber and gold. She looked absolutely ravishing, and I was already regretting my wardrobe choice.

"Damn, girl," I said. "You're a feast for sore eyes. Who needs hors d'oeuvres when the main course is standing right here in front of me."

"That can be arranged," she said. "Come on in. Let's freshen up before heading over to the reception."

Heather motioned me into her room and I stepped inside. As I suspected, her room was larger than mine, with a small sitting room next to her bed and French doors leading out to a balcony.

"I knew I should have upgraded to a suite," I frowned. "I'm already beginning to feel claustrophobic in my tiny little cabin."

I looked out her French doors toward the open bay.

"Do you mind if I check out your view?"

"Of course. Make yourself comfortable. You're welcome to hang at my place anytime you're feeling closed in. I'll just be a couple more minutes."

Heather disappeared into the washroom, and I slid the side doors open and stepped out onto her balcony. I could smell the fresh salty air from the sea and I closed my eyes as I breathed it in.

This is definitely the way to travel, I thought. *Next time,* I reminded myself, *remember to get a full-size suite with balcony.*

After a few minutes, Heather emerged from the washroom looking even more beautiful than before, and I couldn't help shaking my head.

"I'm feeling terribly overdressed. You look like you're getting in the swing of this nude cruise thing already. Should I find something skimpier to wear?"

"Nonsense," Heather said. "You look perfect." Her eyes traced a line down to my aroused nipples protruding against my blouse. "You're revealing just the right amount for the meet and greet. I guarantee you'll be getting a lot of attention in that tight outfit."

I glanced down at her tanned legs and sandals.

"But you're showing a lot more...skin. Am I going to be the only one covering up my whole body?"

"Not at all. Most first-timers come to the initial reception dressed pretty conservative. It takes a couple of days for people to get comfortable being in the buff around their fellow passengers. By the second or third day, everybody will be strolling around buck naked. After the reception there's a dance, where the lights get turned down. You'll have plenty of opportunity to shed some of your clothes then."

As Heather walked toward me, I watched her breasts jiggle under her sheer blouse. When she stood in front of me, I stared at her tits and soft brown nipples. I couldn't stop myself.

"May I?" I said, looking gently into her eyes.

"I thought you'd never ask," she smiled.

I lifted her top and cupped her breasts in my hands and squeezed them softly. They were full and firm, and perfectly shaped, straight out of a centerfold. I noticed her areolas contract and her nipples begin to extend. I rolled them gently between my thumbs and forefingers, and she leaned in to kiss me. When our lips met, I pushed my body toward hers and pressed my hips against hers. She grabbed the back of my head and pulled me closer as our tongues danced around each other's mouths. I could have fucked her right then and there, but after a long lingering kiss, she pulled away.

"There'll be plenty of time for this later," she said. "Let's go meet some new people at the reception. This is a *nude cruise*, remember? We don't want to be holed up in our cabin the whole time, do we?"

"I suppose not," I said, slightly disappointed. My head knew she was right, but the ache in my pussy disagreed. I wanted her right now, and I didn't feel like sharing her with anybody else.

"Come on," she said, grabbing my hand, pulling me toward the door. "Let's go trip the night fantastic."

When we got to the top deck, Heather led me to a large open lounge with floor-to-ceiling windows offering a commanding view of the bay. I hadn't realized the ship had already left the pier, and I saw that we were steaming past South Pointe Park toward the open sea.

There were hundreds of people milling around the room, and Heather clasped my hand as she led me toward the bar. I was glad almost everybody was fully clothed, ranging from shorts and T-shirts to camisoles and bikini bottoms. A few veteran Fantasy Cruise travelers had been bold enough to go topless, but for the most part, it was a fairly low-key affair.

"What'll you have, ladies?" a handsome bartender wearing a white dress shirt and bowtie asked.

"I'll have a watermelon vodka," I said.

"I'd like some sex on the beach please," Heather said.

"Coming right up," the bartender smiled.

"You're so naughty," I teased Heather.

"Hey, when in Rome..." she said.

I turned and looked around the room. Heather had given me good advice about what to wear, and I began to feel more relaxed.

"You were right about the dress code tonight," I said. "Though the bartender seems a little formal. Are the staff always dressed so prim and proper?"

"They're always *dressed*, if that's what you mean. It's company policy that staff always must wear clothes, even on a nude cruise. Something about maintaining their professionalism, I suppose. It kind of helps to separate the staff from the guests, especially when you need something. The officers dress in navy whites, and the servers typically wear black pants, vests, and bow ties."

I watched the bartender approach us as he returned from the other end of the bar.

"Are they allowed to...you know...*hook up* with guests?" I asked.

"Officially it's a no-no, but whatever enterprising staff chooses to do when they're off duty, is nobody's business. If they get caught cavorting with passengers they can technically be fired, but it's pretty hard not to dip your toe in the water every now and then with so many flirty naked passengers floating around."

"I see your point," I said, as a pretty topless girl walked past us.

"Here you go, ladies," the bartender said, placing our drinks in front of us.

"Come on," Heather said, picking up her glass. "Let's go mingle."

For the next hour or so, Heather and I stuck together as we wandered from one cluster of passengers to another, making small talk. Nobody seemed to want to address the elephant in the room, mostly sticking with safe subjects like where we were from, what we did for a living, and if we'd been on a Fantasy Cruise before.

But everybody was definitely checking each other out. Although most of us were technically fully 'dressed', there was plenty enough skin showing to get a good idea of what we'd look like naked. Most of the men wore tight T-shirts or open shirts, revealing plenty of chiseled pecs and abs. The women wore skimpy bikinis, or flimsy camisoles and miniskirts. It was a feast for the eyes, and I soaked it all in. After a little while, I spotted the tall gentleman who I'd made eye contact with in the security line, and I gently steered Heather in his direction.

"I see you managed to survive the security gauntlet," he said to me, as I shimmied up next to him.

"Barely," I laughed. "I wasn't sure who was going to arrest me first —the security guards for my smuggled contraband or the passengers who were steaming about me holding up the line."

"It wasn't so bad," he smiled. "Traveling on a ship is easier than a plane. Is this your first time?"

"Yes," I said. "How about you?"

"This is my second trip. I guess I had some unfinished business from my first time around. There's so much to do on this big ship— one week hardly seems to be enough time to take it all in."

I paused for a moment as I appraised his body. He was wearing creme-colored linen pants and sandals, with a loose-fitting short-sleeved Bermuda shirt. But it was unbuttoned enough to show the cleft rippling between his chiseled pecs as he motioned with his powerful arms. His dark eyes beckoned to me, as I began to fantasize about falling into his arms.

"I'm Marc," he said, extending his hand.

"Jade," I said, feeling his large fingers envelop me. I turned toward Heather. "And this is my partner in crime, Heather."

Marc smiled as he looked at Heather, trying to keep his gaze concentrated above her barely concealed breasts.

"Are you two sisters?" he said. "Because I have seen such a lovely pair since Giselle and Patricia Bundchen."

"If you're talking about Jade and me," Heather teased, "no." Then she grabbed her breasts and shook them provocatively. "But if you're talking about my girls here, I'll take that as a compliment."

"Either way," Marc said, "I mean it as a compliment."

A woman's voice suddenly came over the room's public address system to break the sexual tension. The three of us turned toward the stage, where a woman wearing white shorts and a pressed shirt was standing holding a mic.

"Good evening, Fantasy Cruise travelers!" she said, raising her voice in welcome.

A loud cheer filled the room from the attending guests.

"My name's Ashley, and I'll be your cruise director. For those of you who are traveling on your maiden voyage with Fantasy Cruise, welcome. And for those of you returning for more fun and games, I promise you won't be disappointed. We've added even more fantasy activities to uplift and stimulate you.

"All of you should have found the brochure with our full Fantasy Menu on your nightstand when you checked into your staterooms, but we have lots more here on the desk beside the stage. Whenever you have any questions, just come see me any time. I'll be here the rest of the evening, and you can find my office mid-ship next to the Poseidon Restaurant on Deck B. Or just ring me at triple-two on your in-room phone.

"But now, let's get this party started with our first Fantasy Dance!" she hollered.

The suddenly lights dimmed and flashing lights began circulating the room. The sound of Marvin Gaye's *Let's Get it On* began booming over the speakers, and Heather, Marc and I began swaying our hips together in unison. Heather turned toward me and began shaking her ass suggestively in Marc's direction.

He's dreamy! she mouthed to me.

Damn straight, I returned, widening my eyes in agreement.

Marc simply smiled at me as he pretended to grind his hips against Heather's ass.

My first fantasy cruise was off to a promising start.

4

GETTING DOWN

For the next hour or so, Heather, Marc and I got our groove on as the swirling lights from the disco ball flashed over the writhing crowd. With the sun beginning to set over the horizon, the room became increasingly dark, and some brave passengers began shedding their clothes. Heather was the first to take off her skimpy top, and after another ten minutes of bumping and grinding with her and Marc, I soon followed suit. Not long after, Marc ripped off his shirt and threw it on a growing pile beside the stage.

It felt fabulous to be semi-nude, and we shamelessly rubbed our bodies together as the sexy music played in the background. It didn't take long for us to remove our clothes completely as we got more and more worked up by the suggestive lyrics. When Donna Summer's *Love to Love You Baby* came over the speakers, we moved in close and rolled our hips and chests together, our passion rising in tandem with the singer's orgiastic moans. I could feel Marc's cock hardening against our bodies as my wetness commingled with Heather's on our skin. As usual, Heather made the first move.

"Let's get out of here," she panted in our ears, and we didn't even bother to pick up our clothes as the three of us pranced out of the lounge. Bypassing the elevator, Heather led the way down the closest stairwell while we raced down the three flights to E deck. We giggled our way down the hall past a few other half-dressed passengers as we headed toward Heather's room. When we got to her door, I looked at her blankly, wondering how we were going to get in. We were all stark naked, and none of us were carrying a room key.

"Shit!" I said to Heather. "What now? Maybe we can find a secluded spot on the deck—"

"Not to worry," she said. "I've been in this predicament before, and I've taken precautions."

She kneeled down on the floor and peered through the small crack under the base of her door. Then she reached into the space with her fingers and pulled a credit-card-sized room key out across the carpet.

"Shazam!" she said, standing up and displaying her room key triumphantly. "A lady is prepared for every contingency."

She fumbled with the key in the lock then pushed open the door, and the three of us scrambled into her room. As soon as the door closed, Heather jumped up onto Marc and threw her legs around his hips. He turned and pinned her against the door, and they started kissing passionately. I rubbed my breasts against his sweaty back and moved my hand between his legs. I could feel his hard cock pointing down between Heather's legs, and I rubbed it against her soaking pussy. It didn't take long for the three of us to be coated in her slippery juices.

I squeezed Marc's balls gently as he contracted his glutes and pressed harder against Heather. All three of us were panting, wanting a piece of his meat. Suddenly, he swung around and carried Heather toward the bed with her still clinging to his hips. He placed one knee on the bed and lowered her onto its surface, then pressed his body against hers. Not wanting to interrupt their rhythm, I stood and watched as my sticky hand moved between my legs.

At this point, I was so turned on I could have come just watching Heather and Marc make love. But Heather had other plans, and she twisted her body and flipped Marc over, straddling his hips. She motioned for me to join them on the bed and I kneeled down beside her and kissed her on her lips. I could feel her body writhing over Marc's midsection, and I ran my hands down her stomach to feel their connection. Marc's hard cock was flat against his stomach as Heather rolled back and forth over it with her wet pussy. I played with her clit and she began to moan in my mouth.

Then she began lowering herself until our mouths were inches away from Marc's throbbing phallus. She swung her leg over to Marc's opposite side and his penis popped up into an acute sixty-degree angle, pointing toward his head. In the soft moonlight streaming through Heather's balcony doors, I could see that it was large, straight, and magnificent. The head glistened with a mixture of pre-cum and Heather's juices, and we both wrapped our fingers around it.

While we gave him a slow, two-handed massage, Marc sighed and thrust his manhood into our pliant hands. After a couple of minutes, Heather lowered her head and took him into her mouth, as I cupped his balls and played with the space between his testicles and anus. Marc moaned and began to roll his hips more aggressively, obviously enjoying Heather's attention on his cock. I could hear his passion rising and I began to feel his balls tighten and rise up. I knew it wouldn't take long for him to come with the combined effect of two beautiful women attending to his erogenous area.

Heather must have sensed it too because she lifted her head off his dick and leaned over and kissed me. Marc began to raise himself up wanting to get in on the action, but Heather extended her right hand and pushed him back onto the bed. He quickly got the message and watched the two of us while we explored each other's bodies. I cupped Heather's tits again and rolled her nipples between my fingers, then we pressed our chests together and tribbed our nipples while we fucked each other's mouths with our tongues.

By this time, all three of us were ready for some direct stimulation, and I hesitated, unsure where to go next. It was my first time in a threesome—at least one where I had this degree of control—and I didn't want to leave anyone hanging. Heather suddenly lifted her right leg and swung it over Marc's stomach, then did the same with her other leg until she was straddling his hips from the side. She motioned for me to do the same, then we pulled each other forward until our vulvas touched Marc's throbbing member on opposite sides. It was an incredible sensation feeling the heat of his hard cock sandwiched between our two pussies. Heather and I wasted no time moving our hips up and down, giving Marc an entirely new type of erotic massage.

The three of us were now getting direct stimulation, and Heather and I moaned in each other's mouths as we rubbed our soaking pussies together against Marc's pointed cock. I could feel our combined wetness running between my legs, as I pushed harder against Marc's warm and wonderful joystick. I wrapped my arms around Heather's waist and pulled her closer toward me. By now, we were all moaning in abandon and nearing the tipping point. I tilted my hips downward a bit and pressed my clit against the side of Marc's cock. Heather and I were humping him hard now, and our tits rubbed together as sweat streamed down our stomachs. This was an entirely new kind of tribbing that I'd never experienced before, and the image of the three of us joined together soon put me over the edge.

I threw my head back and let out a primal scream as Heather and I thrashed our hips together and gushed all over Marc's throbbing hard-on. We kissed for another minute as we came down from our high, then we separated and peered at Marc. He had a silly smile on his face, but his cock was still pointing up, bobbing gently over his stomach from the pulse flowing through its veins. I ran my hand over my stomach to see if I could detect any sign of semen on me, then I looked at Heather and shook my head to signal that he hadn't come yet.

"Good boy," she said, leaning over to give him a long, lingering kiss.

Then she shifted her body until her hips were behind his head, and she looked at me, silently nodding. I knew her intent immediately, and I swung my legs over Marc's midsection, straddling his hips in her direction. She lifted herself up, placing her pussy over his face, then lowered herself onto his eager mouth. I could see her eyes roll back in her head as he took her swollen clit between his lips and began to suck her, and she began to grind her hips into his face.

I didn't need any more encouragement. I grabbed Marc's thick schlong and directed the tip toward my quivering opening. I teased him for just a second, rubbing his sticky head against my clit and vulva, then I lowered myself onto him until his mound pressed firmly against my clit. As Heather and I locked eyes, I convulsed in a mini-orgasm.

It was an unbelievably hot sight watching each other fuck this adonis from opposite ends as we watched our passion rising. I began to rock my hips in unison with Heather, and I could feel Marc's hips answering the call. I loved the feeling of his big cock filling me up, and he knew how to move his hips to give my clit direct stimulation. The combined feeling of my clit grinding into his mound and the head of his cock rubbing against my G-spot was driving me crazy. I began moaning more loudly as I stepped up the pace of my humping action, while Heather and I clasped hands.

I wanted to make this last as long as I could, but the sights and sounds of three beautiful people joining together in an erotic union was too much. I could feel my orgasm welling deep inside me and I made one final push down hard onto Marc's cock as I squeezed Heather's hands like a vice. When I finally came, I grunted like a wild animal as my body spasmed over Marc's hips while I looked Heather straight in her eyes.

I guess that was too much for Marc too, because he grabbed my hips with two hands and thrust his hips into the air, lifting me off the mattress as I felt his cock throbbing in rhythmic contractions inside my pussy. With him moaning into her pussy and her seeing me have a powerful orgasm, it soon put Heather over the edge. Just as I was beginning to feel the last of my contractions subside, her hands squeezed mine hard and her eyelids narrowed as she clamped her thighs around Marc's head. She growled like a dog in heat as I watched the pleasure roll over her pretty face. The whole time we never took our eyes off one another.

When she finally collected her breath and came down from her orgasm, she smiled at me. We were both thinking the same thing. My new partner in crime and I had found our first accomplice.

WATER SPORTS

Later that evening, Marc returned to his room and Heather and I continued to make love into the wee hours. By 3:00 a.m., we were both spent, and we fell asleep sprawled naked atop the bed sheets, as a cool breeze from the ocean wafted over our sweaty bodies. When the morning sun streamed through her balcony door, Heather rolled over and caressed my breast.

"Morning, Sunshine," she said, as my eyes slowly flitted open.

"Morning, Beautiful," I said, moving in closer to give her a kiss.

"That was quite a first night we had together."

"Mmmm, yes," I said, tasting her sweet tongue in my mouth. "Hopefully the first of many."

"I hope so too. But I don't want to steal all your time and attention on this cruise. The main idea is to mix it up and take advantage of as many activities as you can in the limited time you have available."

"Can't we do that together?" I asked.

"Some of them, for sure. But I think some of the other activities you might enjoy more on your own."

"What about our new friend Marc?"

"I'm pretty sure he'll want to get out there on his own and sow some more of his oats. But he left his room number on my nightstand, so we might have a chance to hook up with him again before the cruise is over."

I looked out the open balcony doors at the sun shimmering over the open sea.

"You've done this before. What activity do you recommend we try next?"

"Most people like to ease into this whole nudity thing. Let's head up to the pool and do some people watching while we work on our tans. There's also a cool fountain on the top deck that's quite fun and refreshing. But first, I think we should get something to eat. I don't know about you, but I'm famished!"

"Me too. I think we burned enough calories last night for *three* meals. But first I'd like to return to my cabin to freshen up. What do you recommend I wear to breakfast?"

"It'll be pretty hot up top. A bikini and sandals should be enough. You'll just be taking it all off pretty soon anyway. You don't want to have to carry a bunch of clothes around with you."

"That reminds me," I suddenly remembered. "I've still got to retrieve my stuff from last night in the lounge."

"Something tells me you're not going to need jeans and a blouse for a while. We can pick that up on our return to our cabins later in the day. Did you want to borrow my shawl to get back to your room?"

I smiled at Heather's thoughtfulness.

"I'm just a few doors down. Judging by last night, half the people on the ship are already nude, so a little more streaking down the hall shouldn't hurt me."

"You're going to need a key to get in though. I'm guessing you didn't think of my trick."

Heather leaned over and picked up her room phone then tapped some numbers on the dial.

"Yes," she spoke into the phone, "my friend's lost her key for room E48. Can you send someone down with a replacement? She's in my room, E32. Thank you."

Ten minutes later, there was a soft tap on Heather's door.

"Maybe I'll take you up on that shawl offer after all," I said.

Heather smiled and went to her closet and held the garment open for me as I slid my arms into it.

"Meet you in the Poseidon Restaurant in an hour?" she said.

"Deal," I said, giving her a quick kiss.

I opened the door, gave Heather a playful shake of my ass, then followed the porter back to my room.

***

After breakfast, Heather led me to the main pool on the top deck, where scores of people were lounging naked on deck chairs and playing in the water. A series of interconnected pools simulated the look of a tropical lagoon, complete with life-size palm trees and small cabanas. We found a couple of open lounge chairs not far from the bar, and Heather asked me to mind them for us while she went to get a couple of drinks.

While she was gone, I made a quick scan of the scene. Virtually everybody was already naked, and it was a busy hive of activity. On one end of the lagoon, a large waterslide deposited screaming guests into the splashing water. In an adjacent basin, a small group of people were playing water polo. On the other side of the patio, a few passengers were skipping through a water fountain like a bunch of playful toddlers. It was all pretty surreal, and I paused to take it all in.

"Checking out all the action?" Heather said, returning from the bar and handing me a drink.

"Mmm, yes," I said, taking a sip of my pina colada. "There's certainly a lot of...*diversions*."

"Are you referring to all the naked people or the activities?"

"Both," I said, scanning the bodies of some of the men walking around the pool. "It's strange, though. Everybody seems so...*asexual*. I would have thought more people would be, you know, *aroused*, seeing each other naked."

"That's the thing about us all being in the same boat, so to speak. Like I said earlier, nudity is the great equalizer. Everybody gets used to it pretty quickly, and before you know it they're walking around like it's a normal walk in the park." Heather paused as she appraised my demeanor. "Are you disappointed?"

"Not really. I just expected the men in particular would be showing more sign of, you know, *interest*. The cruise operator billed this as more of a sex cruise than a nude cruise."

Heather smiled, as she lay back on her lounge chair.

"Believe me, there'll be plenty of opportunity for you to get down and dirty on this cruise. There's more going on than might first appear. For instance, take a look at that woman standing in the fountain on the other side of the patio."

I peered across the pool and saw a naked woman in her twenties standing over some jets of water spraying up from the surface. She had a strange look on her face as she spread her legs and squatted over the stream.

"It looks like she's having an enema," I laughed.

"I think she's directing the spray to a *different* part of her body," Heather said.

The look on the woman's face changed to one of pleasure as she began to shimmy her hips over the water stream. Suddenly the spray started pulsing like a shower head, and she let out a low moan.

I crossed my legs, beginning to feel a tingle in my pussy.

"I see what you mean," I said. "Now I see why they call it the Fantasy Fountain."

Heather noticed me squirming on my chair.

"Do you feel like giving it a try?"

"In a sec. Let me enjoy her experience first."

The woman suddenly grabbed her tits with her hands and pushed them up, as the spray from the patio surface gushed up over her abdomen and washed over her face. She was grunting and groaning now and moving her hips more rhythmically over the jet.

"Fuck, that's hot," I said.

"Kind of a nice way to cool off on a hot day like this."

"It looks like it might take the edge off in more ways than one."

Suddenly, the woman began screaming, as her body convulsed and her hips shook in rhythmic spasms. There was no doubt to us or any of the many other spectators that she had just enjoyed a powerful orgasm. When she staggered out of the fountain back toward her lounge chair, a small round of applause rose from around the pool.

"What do you think?" Heather said. "Are you up for it?"

"Now that I know I'm going to have an audience, I wouldn't mind some company. Will you come with me?"

"I think I will," Heather said, winking at me. "Let's toss these bikinis first. We don't want anything getting in the way of all the fun."

Heather nonchalantly unclasped her bikini top behind her back then stepped out of her bottoms. I'd almost forgotten how beautiful she was, and her tanned body looked magnificent in the bright sunshine. Her shaved pussy left nothing to the imagination, and I could see her nub poking out of her labia at the top of her pussy.

"Damn girl," I said, opening my eyes wide. "You're never afraid to let it all hang out."

"It's called a *fantasy cruise*, right? Let's live out our fantasies. Get those clothes off and let's go have some fun!"

I pulled off my top and bottom and threw them on my lounge chair, then Heather and I scampered around the pool past a throng of curious onlookers. When we got in the fountain, it was actually quite refreshing. The water was warm, but it felt cool against my hot skin in the blazing sun. The water jets were spread a few feet apart, facing different directions with alternating pulsing patterns. Some were a constant stream and some stopped and started periodically, while others pulsed at different speeds like an overhead shower faucet.

Heather and I stepped into the sprays and danced around for a minute, laughing and holding hands. Then we came together and kissed, rubbing our bodies together as the spray shot up between us, soaking our faces. Suddenly, I no longer cared about being naked in full view of the other pool guests. I was lost in the deluge of sensations I felt from the water jets spraying against my ass and Heather rubbing her body against mine.

We shifted position until we found a spot in the fountain where a steady stream directed toward our pussies. Then we pushed our mounds together so the stream sprayed directly against our touching clits. I opened my mouth and gasped as Heather smiled at me. This was a once-in-a-lifetime experience, and I wanted to enjoy every moment of it with her.

Suddenly, two more sprays began jetting at a forty-five-degree angle from behind each of us, and we bent our knees to give the spray direct access to our rosebuds.

"Oh my God!" I said to Heather, as my eyes flew open.

"Is this *arousing* enough for you?" she said, grinding her clit against mine.

"Fuck, yes!"

Just when I thought it couldn't get any more intense, the steady spray directed toward our clits began pulsing in strong, flickering streams.

"Uhnn," I moaned, closing my eyes at the intense feeling of pleasure I was experiencing from every part of my body.

"Enjoy, Baby," Heather said, as she thrust her tongue into my mouth, swaying her hips in tandem with mine.

I could feel the passion rising quickly inside me, and there was no way I could hold it back any longer.

"Fuck, I'm coming!" I said, as my pussy clenched inside me and I became weak in the knees. "Ohh, Ohh, Ohh," I panted into Heather's mouth, feeling the waves roll over me. Heather grunted into my mouth and I felt her hips shudder against mine as she reached her own peak. We moaned out loud together as the warm water from the jets sprayed all over our ecstatic faces.

When we finally came down from our orgasms, we held each other over the gentle spray, leaning against one another in exhaustion. When we separated, a loud cheer rose from around the pool from the appreciative crowd.

I guess this won't to be so hard getting used to after all, I thought.

6

PEAK SENSATIONS

Heather and I spent the rest of the day lounging around the pool, people watching. We made a few new friends and got some more cabin numbers, but mostly we just wanted to relax and scope out our next move. Heather said if we didn't pace ourselves, we'd either be too sore or exhausted to partake in some of the more adventurous shipboard activities. After perusing the ship's Fantasy Menu, we both agreed our next rendezvous would be at the climbing wall.

I went back to my cabin alone that night planning to get a good night's sleep, with visions of naked climbers exposing themselves as they scaled the cliff. I woke up refreshed the next morning, eager to try out the next erotic challenge. When I met Heather at the breakfast buffet, the room was filled with naked passengers filling their plates with hardly a sideways glance. I guess she'd been right about everybody getting comfortable being in the nude by the third day.

As she explained to me what to expect at the climbing wall, my eyes widened in anticipation. It sounded terrifying and exciting at the same time.

"Do people ever *fall*?" I asked.

"Everyone's strapped into a harness and they have spotters to maintain tension on the rope holding you up, so even if you do slip, it's perfectly safe."

I frowned at the thought of other people watching my naked body from below.

"So I'll have some stranger watching my bare ass as I stretch my legs and move up the wall?"

"Yes, but that's part of the fun of it. Knowing other people are watching you as you get higher and higher is quite titillating, for both you and the observers. Plus, the staff doing the rope work are usually pretty buff, so it's kind of hot."

The idea of exposing my body while I stimulated myself on the wall reminded me of my Dinner Party experience. I squirmed in my seat reflecting back on the memory of Jasmine playing with me under the table while my fellow diners looked on.

"Tell me more about the unique 'features' on the wall."

"Besides the usual cup and lip-shaped ledges for gaining a comfortable hand and foot hold, there are other more *erotic* holds to clasp onto along the way."

"Such as?"

"For starters, some of the lips vibrate, so you can pause and get a little extra stimulation whenever you're feeling in the mood."

I pictured the idea of being in a harness clinging to a wall while sex toys stimulated my private parts.

"Now I see why they strap you in," I said. "I could barely maintain my balance on solid ground at the fountain yesterday, the more worked up I got. I can imagine how weak in the knees people might get, stimulated in a similar manner while climbing a challenging wall."

"Exactly," Heather said. "Especially the higher you go. The stimulation gets more and more intense the higher you climb."

"How so?"

"The features start out pretty tame at the bottom, just little nodules to rub against. But then they start vibrating, like little magic bullets. They get progressively larger and more animated the higher you go. If you make it all the way to the top, they've got some full-size dildos that twist and rotate to really give you a ride."

"Mmm," I said, feeling the moisture beginning to build inside my pussy. "Just like my favorite rabbit vibrator."

"Kind of like that. Except this time, you're suspended twenty-five feet off the ground in full view of your spotter and any other spectators while you get off."

Suddenly I had a burning need to have something inside me.

"That sounds pretty hot."

Heather raised her eyebrows and nodded.

"There's something about the whole idea that's very arousing. I think you'll find it's quite a different experience."

I wrinkled my forehead as I pondered the possibilities.

"What about the guys? Are there similar erotic features for *them* to enjoy on the wall?"

"Definitely. The wall holds alternate between 'innies' and 'outies', so everybody has a chance to enjoy. Many of them are fashioned in the form of flexible lips, pussies, and anuses, where men can insert their dongs along the way and get a similar thrill. Near the top, they become animated with internal vibrators, just like the bullets and dildos for the ladies. It's quite arousing to watch the men and women stop and fuck the life-like features along the way."

I shook my head and grimaced at a new thought.

"What about all the...*by-products* deposited along the way? It must get pretty slippery and gross before long. I wouldn't want to place my hands or my pussy anywhere near some dude's day-old cum."

Heather scrunched her nose and laughed.

"Not to worry. The ship operators have got it all figured out. After every new climber comes down from the wall, they cover the wall in a tarp and wash it down with high-powered steam water jets. They keep it all very antiseptic."

I clenched my legs together, trying to stimulate my burning clit. I couldn't wait to give it a try.

"What do you say?" Heather said. "Are you up for it?"

"Definitely. My pussy's ready to climb on just about anything right now!"

- - -

When we got to the wall, I was surprised by how tall it was. It towered at least thirty feet straight up, with foot and hand holds separated a few feet apart. It was odd but strangely arousing to see the artificial vulvas and dildos sticking out from its surface. Two naked people were already strapped into hip harnesses at the base of the wall, a man and a woman both appearing to be in their mid-20s.

They spoke with familiarity to one another, so I assumed they were a couple. What a thrill I thought it must be for the pair to experience this together. A small crowd of friends and onlookers were gathered a few feet further back from the wall, egging the couple on. As Heather had described, two buff staff members held thick ropes in their hands, which looped up over an extended wheel at the top of the structure. The other end dangled down the front of the facade and clasped securely to the front of their harnesses.

"Are you ready?" the man said, looking at his partner.

She nodded silently, then reached up for the first handhold and placed her foot onto a lip at the base of the wall. Heather looked at me and smiled. The idea of doing this in tandem appealed to me, and I hoped that the two of us would have our turn soon. It was strange watching the climbers spread their legs and bend their asses as they stretched to reach the next higher holds. I could see the man's balls hanging between his thighs and his penis wobbling back and forth as he swung from one placement to the other. They both seemed so focused on figuring out their path of ascent that they barely paused to rest.

But about half way up, the woman suddenly paused and pushed her hips against the wall. I could see a small ball-shaped object resting between her thighs, nestled against her vulva. A gentle vibrating noise emanated from the area. She looked over at her partner and smiled, encouraging him to find a similar place to rest.

He glanced to his left and saw an orange ring protruding from the wall. He stepped up and over until his cock was level with the ring then he positioned his flaccid member inside the hole. Suddenly the ring started vibrating, and the man threw his head back. I could see his cock hardening and lengthening as he positioned the vibrating ring around the glans of his penis. He turned toward his partner and they giggled while they gently humped the wall together.

"Higher! Higher!" their friends urged them on from the bottom of the wall.

The two reluctantly disengaged from their fixed positions and resumed their climb up the wall. About five feet higher up, the woman came upon a curved rubber dildo protruding about three inches from the surface, and she paused over it then lowered her pussy until it disappeared inside her hole. She started humping the small dildo to cheers from the crowd. I was glad everybody's attention was focused on the wall, because my fingers had already begun circling my clit as I matched the woman's hip movements.

The man noticed a new feature on his side of the wall, this time mimicking the lips and tongue of a woman. He didn't hesitate to slip his now fully erect cock inside the orifice and begin to moan as he deep-throated his artificial lover. Both he and his partner began speeding up the movement of their hips and it looked like one or both of them might come soon. But the crowd at the base of the wall weren't quite ready.

"Get to the pussy and the dick at the top!" someone shouted. "You're almost there!"

The couple glanced at one another then looked down and shook their heads in mock frustration. Then they peered up the wall and resumed their climb. All the while, the two staff members holding the ropes held the lines taut while pretending to be uninterested in the actions of the climbers. But I noticed the telltale bulge in their pants that belied their disinterest. I looked over at Heather and saw that her hand had slipped between her legs too.

The couple picked up their climbing speed with new determination, and it didn't take long for them to near the top of the wall, where the woman was presented with a large purple dildo and the man with a gaping artificial pussy. The woman placed her lips around the dildo and pretended to give it blowjob while the man pushed his face into the artificial vulva and shook his head playfully. The crowd below erupted in a loud cheer.

"Fuck it! Fuck it! Fuck it!" they chanted in unison.

The woman climbed a few feet higher, then placed the big dildo inside her pussy, and relaxed her legs. The staff member holding her rope bent his knees, clasping the end of the rope tightly with two hands. He'd obviously been in this situation before, and he braced himself for the shifting load. Just a few feet away on the other side of the wall, the man positioned himself adjacent to the artificial vulva and inserted his dick into the hole.

"Whomp! Whomp! Whomp!" chanted their friends down below, in encouragement.

With everybody's attention focused on the wall, Heather suddenly moved behind me and squeezed my breast with one hand, while she slipped her fingers inside my cunny from behind. I could hear vibrating sounds emanating from the artificial pussy and dildo, and the man and the woman clenched their buttocks as they began to fuck their sex toys more vigorously. They peered over at one another and mouthed something, and I could hear their breathing escalating in urgency.

Heather began to speed up the pace of her ministrations, and I fucked her fingers as I pretended it was me on the wall. Within a minute or so, the couple's bodies began convulsing, and their arms and legs suddenly became rigid. Heather held me tightly while I clamped down hard on her hand as I came at the same time with the couple on the wall.

The handlers held the couple's lines firmly until they pushed away from the edifice and were gently lowered. When they got to the bottom and removed their harnesses, their friends surrounded them in a group hug, jumping up and down in celebration. The staff ordered everybody to step ten feet back from the wall, then a canvas tarp descended from the top and hot jets began cleaning the surface.

I could feel the steam rising above the tarp as a rivulet of water began pooling at the base of the structure, draining into a grated hole beside the podium.

I turned around and looked at Heather. She raised her eyebrows to signal if I was game to try it next. I simply nodded my head and smiled. I could feel my own rivulet of warm liquid running down my legs.

7

HOUSE OF HOLES

After they finished sanitizing the wall, Heather and I took our turn on it. Most of the spectators had moved on after the previous couple came down, but it was still unnerving being watched so closely by our rope handlers. As usual, Heather took the lead sitting over the erotic extrusions, and the look of delight on her face soon encouraged me to do the same. We came multiple times grinding our pussies into the various devices, culminating with two powerful orgasms on the large dildos at the top of the wall.

We spent a few more hours lounging around the pool, then Heather encouraged me to strike out on my own. I protested briefly, still not entirely comfortable with the idea of engaging in public sex by myself, but she suggested a few venues that might provide an opportunity for more privacy. After a quick lunch, I reluctantly began exploring the ship.

My first stop was the Sexy Games Room. It was filled with various contraptions, where solo men and women were getting fucked by automated machines. At one station, a woman bent over on all fours, while a large plastic dildo pounded in and out of her pussy. At another one, a man sat on a chair humping a life-like silicone doll, while he squeezed her fake tits and thrust his tongue into her fellatio-shaped mouth. In the corner of the room, a pretty co-ed straddled a device that looked like a pommel horse, as she bucked and writhed atop its vibrating saddle.

It all seemed so surreal and impersonal for me. I wanted a *human* connection, like the one Heather and I shared at the fantasy fountain. I scanned the activity menu and considered going for an Intimate Massage, thinking at least this way I'd have some human touch, and then I remembered one of Heather's recommendations. The description for the House of Holes sounded intriguing:

Hook up with a stranger on the other side of a wall through your own personal intimate portal. You can choose to 'give', 'receive', or 'merge' with a partner of either sex in an erotic and completely anonymous connection. Or you can choose to simply watch, as other couples get their groove on in this sensuous and erotic 'House of Holes'.

Yes, I thought, *'merging' with a partner is exactly what I need.* The notion of engaging with someone through my own personal 'glory hole', reminded me of the fun I'd had playing with hidden strangers in the Dark Room.

When I got to the venue and opened the door, the first thing I noticed was the sound. A cacophony of moans and grunts greeted me, as a variety of naked men and women shimmied their hips, asses, and mouths against the vinyl-coated walls. The lights were dimmed, but I could see the unmistakable shape of erect penises and vulvas poking through various small holes scattered around the room.

People on the other side were shaking their hips trying to get the attention of someone from inside the room, but everybody was already engaged in some form of coupling. One man was humping the wall, being serviced by someone from the other side. Another one kneeled on the floor giving head to a well-endowed fellow who thrust his cock vigorously into his consort's eager mouth. Not far away, a woman bent over rubbing her ass against the wall, where another man plunged his cock through the hole into her pussy.

But the whole scene somehow left me cold. It struck me as cheap and dirty. Medical clearance or not, I couldn't get on board with the idea of connecting with some other stranger's private parts in such an impersonal way. Just as I was about to leave the room, I noticed a neon sign in the corner reading 'Private View Rooms'.

Private definitely sounded more appealing. And being able to *see* my partner was more along my lines.

I opened the door and entered a dimmed hall with closed doors lining both sides. Most of them were locked with a sign reading 'Occupied', but a little further down the hall I found one marked 'Vacant'. I turned the handle and stepped into a small room. It had a single vinyl chair facing a floor-to-ceiling glass wall with a one-foot diameter hole cut in the middle. On the other side of the glass was a similar room with an empty chair.

I turned and locked my door, then checked the chair to see if it was clean. There were no visible marks or residue, but I ran my hand over its smooth surface just to be sure. Even the vinyl floor looked like it had just been cleaned, reflecting the light from the single over-head incandescent lamp.

At least they clean up after themselves pretty well, I nodded, as I sat down on the chair and waited for someone to enter the adjacent room.

I expected a man looking for a simulated adult video store glory hole experience, but I was pleasantly surprised when a slim young Asian girl opened the door. She paused for a moment and appraised me seated in my chair with my legs slightly ajar, then she turned around and locked her door from the inside. She was carrying something but she kept it hidden from my view as she turned around.

We could have easily talked if we'd wanted to, with a large enough hole in the glass to carry on a private conversation. But we both seemed to want to just *look* for the time being. She sat down on her chair and placed the hidden object behind her, then spread her legs apart. She had a petite figure with firm B-cup breasts and a small V-shaped patch of pubic hair on her mound that pointed toward a protruding nub at the top of her labia. She had large eyes with long lashes, and she smiled at me as she began to run her hands over her body.

I watched her for a moment, as I felt the juices from my pussy puddle on the chair in front of me. She placed her hands on the inside of her thighs and pulled them slowly toward her apex, then continued moving them up toward her chest. She squeezed her tits then pushed them up and tilted her head down, sucking each of her nipples.

I wanted a piece of her so badly, but I was enjoying her little striptease. I cupped my left breast with one hand and I began to play with my clit with my other, spreading my legs further apart. She did the same and pointed her toes, as she opened her mouth, signaling her pleasure. I could hear a soft moan emanating through the hole in the glass as she flitted her eyes and began to rock her hips on her chair.

By now I was thoroughly soaked, feeling the intensity rising in my loins. I slipped the fingers from my other hand into my pussy as I rubbed my clit more forcefully. The Asian girl suddenly thrust both of her hands into her love box and began fucking herself with a two-handed motion, rocking her chest in tandem with her hips. The sound of her juices sloshing around as she finger-fucked herself with both hands ratcheted my excitement up another level.

I could feel my orgasm beginning to build as I let out a low moan. The girl spread her legs wider until they were virtually straight out to her sides. I marveled at her flexibility, reminding me of my naked yoga experience with Kayla and Neve. We were groaning in tandem as we each fucked our own pussies, alternating our line of sight between our sopping pussies and our glazed-over eyes. Suddenly the girl's chest began to heave, and she grunted a staccato burst of moans as she hunched over in orgasmic spasms. That was enough to put me over the edge, and I growled like a wild animal as I gushed all over the chair in front of me. It was incredibly erotic watching each other come with only a few feet separating us between the clear pane of glass.

But now I was ready for a more personal connection. After I came down from my high, I stood up and walked toward the glass and motioned for her to do the same. She walked slowly toward the hole in the partition, then placed her palms flat against the glass at shoulder height. She was even prettier up close, with big brown eyes, high cheekbones, and full pouty lips. I placed my hands over hers and we moved our faces toward the glass until our lips touched on the cool surface. There was something about being this close to another naked woman and not being able to touch her that I found highly arousing.

Our opposite hands traced a path down the side of the glass and we reached through the hole to touch each other's pussies. I groaned when I felt the heat of her box and her fingers touching my clit. We lowered our bodies a few more inches to gain better access to our midsections while still peering into one another's eyes. I stuck out my tongue and began to lick the glass, showing that I was ready for a more personal touch.

I bent my knees a little further and her fingers slipped out of me as I squatted down over the hole in front of her pussy. She pushed her hips into the glass to try to give me better access, but it felt awkward tilting my head through the hole trying to get to her clit with my tongue. Sensing my frustration, she suddenly stepped back from the glass then lifted her right leg straight up and placed her heel against the glass beside her shoulder. Then she pushed her body forward until her legs were pressed flat against the glass in a perfect split.

Her open vulva was now pushing through the hole directly toward my face. I didn't hesitate to take her little button into my mouth and roll it around my tongue like a peppermint candy. Her lubrication coated my face as she ground her pussy against my cheeks. I reached through the hole and wrapped my arm around her hips, pulling her harder toward me. She moaned softly and whimpered as she fucked my face. I inserted two fingers into her love canal as I sucked and flicked her little cocklet in my mouth. Then I curled my fingers in a come-hither motion against her G-spot and she bent her knees, pressing her pussy harder against my face and fingers. Her moans were growing in intensity and my heart raced at the idea of her coming on my face. I pushed my fingers deeper inside and circled her clit more quickly with my tongue. Suddenly, she howled as her pussy clamped over my fingers in a long series of hard contractions. I held my face still while she gushed all over me.

If I could have squeezed my whole body through the narrow opening in the glass, I would have pounced on her right then and there and tribbed her hard until we both came together. Instead, I slowly raised myself up until my face was at the same level as hers and kissed her gently against the glass. She smiled at me and blinked twice as if to say 'thank you'. Then she turned around and walked toward the chair and picked up the object which she'd gone to such pains to hide from me. She held it up in the dim light and smiled. It was a long two-sided flexible dildo, anatomically correct on both ends, shaped like a two-headed penis.

Fuck, yes, I thought. *That's what I'm talking about.*

I wanted to fuck this girl so badly, and the two-sided dildo was just what the doctor ordered. She walked up to the glass and held it up in front of me, then licked it up and down the shaft. Then she placed one end in her mouth and simulated fellatio over the silicone glans.

Please, I mouthed through the glass. *I need it inside of me now.*

Demonstrating my urgency, I turned around and placed my ass against the open hole, then bent over to present my open pussy to her. She pushed the dildo through the hole and rubbed it back and forth across my vulva, and I shuddered in pleasure. I bucked my hips against the phallus and pressed my ass harder against the glass, signaling that I wanted her to place it inside me.

When she finally did, I almost fainted in pleasure. The feeling of the thick dildo pushing inside me from behind was exquisite. She pushed it as far as it would go, then I felt some slack on the device as she turned around and faced her ass toward me. I didn't need to look to know what she was doing, as I felt the pressure of the dildo when she pushed the other end inside her own pussy.

When our buttocks touched through the open glass, we groaned as we began to simultaneously fuck the giant phallus. I could feel her juices coating the dildo on the other end as our pussies sloshed and bucked against our imaginary partner. The girl began to whimper as we ground our asses together, trying to come over the thick joystick between our legs. It didn't take long for us to reach our peak as we screamed and shook in simultaneous orgasms on the writhing snake embedded inside us.

It took us over a minute before we were ready to disengage, when the girl finally separated herself from the two-headed dildo and pulled it out of my throbbing pussy. I turned around and placed my lips against the glass, and we kissed one last time before she silently picked up the dildo and exited the room. No words had been necessary the entire time we shared our intimate connection.

Just as I was turning to leave, a buff young man entered the room the girl had just left. I took one look at his large swinging cock and shook my head.

I wouldn't mind a taste of the real thing, I thought.

8

STRAIGHT FLUSH

After I had another go with my new partner in the private view room, I staggered back to my room, sore and exhausted. I slept like a log that night, dreaming of animated cocks and pussies attached to life-like trees, as I walked through a magical forest. When I woke up in the morning, I lay in a giant wet spot atop my leaking cunny and rubbed another one out before showering and heading upstairs to meet Heather for breakfast.

She laughed when I told her about my strange dream, and we entertained each other over lox and pineapple with stories of our experiences from the previous day. She seemed interested in my private view room encounter, but when I told her about my disappointment with the games room, her ears perked up.

"You didn't explore the *other* games rooms?" she said.

"What other games rooms? I only found the one with the holes in the wall."

"There are lots of others that you might find interesting. One of my favorites is the Card Lounge."

"What happens there?"

"It's where groups of people meet to play card games."

"That doesn't sound very interesting."

"It *is* when everybody's naked and they play by different rules."

Heather noticed Marc heading back from the buffet and motioned for him to join them. Virtually everybody was now walking around the ship completely naked, paying little mind to the jiggling breasts and penises as people went about their daily routines.

"Good morning, ladies," Marc said, as he approached our table. "How have you found your shipboard experience so far?"

I took a good long look at Marc's body before he sat down, refreshing my memory from our first night together. Standing well over six feet tall, his well-muscled torso and arms rippled in the bright light streaming through the windows on the top deck. His penis was flaccid, but still hanging a healthy five to six inches as it swung gently above his nicely shaved balls. I picked a thick piece of pineapple from my plate, remembering what his dick felt like standing straight up.

"I think the word is...*eclectic*," I said, sucking the dripping fruit between my lips.

Marc sat down quickly on the other side of our booth to hide his growing erection and smiled.

"There's certainly no shortage of diversions," he said, scooping a large forkful of scrambled eggs into his mouth. "Have you had a favorite experience?"

"You mean besides our little tryst with you?" Heather said, grabbing a sausage from his plate and biting it in half.

"Of course I knew that would be your highlight," Marc said, continued the tease. "I was referring to the venues."

"The climbing wall was fun," Heather said. "But I think Jade may have experienced a different kind of high in one of the private view rooms yesterday."

"Oh? You like those sexy holes, do you?"

"Some holes were a little sexier than others," I said.

"Jade found the rest of the games room a bit underwhelming. I was suggesting she try her hand at a little strip poker. Care to join us after breakfast?"

"Just the three of us?" Marc said.

"I think we need a plus-one to balance things out. Maybe we can persuade one of the guys from the House of Holes to take his dick out of the wall and find a more interesting use for it."

Marc stretched his lips and nodded.

"Game on," he said, finishing his sausage and eggs.

W hen we got to the card room, we saw an empty round glass table with a pack of playing cards and four trays of betting chips. Heather excused herself for a moment, then returned a few minutes later holding a college-age boy's hand. He looked a little perplexed as he stared at the three of us and the empty table.

"*Three's* a lot more fun than one, don't you think?" she said to the young man. "Plus, there's no barriers here to limit your engagement. Are you ready to play some sexy games?"

He paused for a moment, then stuck out his hand.

"I'm Liam," he said, signaling his assent.

After we all introduced ourselves, we took alternating seats at the table and Heather cracked open the pack of cards.

"What are we playing?" Liam enquired.

"Five card stud," Heather said, winking at me. "With two *real* studs. You *do* know how to play poker, Liam?"

"Yes, but what are the stakes? I didn't bring any money..."

"You're so cute," Heather said. "We're not playing for money. We're playing for *favors*. The rule is that whoever wins each hand, gets to command one or more of us to perform some kind of act. Whoever ends up with the most chips at the end of the hour gets to propose a special group activity. The only limitation is that no one is allowed to come until the very end."

"That makes it a little more interesting," Marc said.

"And challenging," Liam said, crossing his legs to hide his growing erection under the table.

"Right then," Heather said, pulling two red chips from her tray. "The ante is ten dinars."

"Dinars?" Liam said.

"It's just *play* money, remember? They gain *real* value a little later."

Heather dealt one card face down to each player then one more face up. We each looked at our hole cards and placed our bets. Liam placed the largest stake in the pile, then Heather dealt another set of cards face up. Liam showed two Kings and threw in one of his three black chips.

"Too steep for me," Marc huffed, pushing his cards into the waste pile.

Heather displayed two tens, and I had a Jack-high.

Heather matched Liam's bet, and I decided to fold. She dealt the fourth card to herself and Liam. Heather got a Queen, while Liam showed an Ace.

"Hooo!" Marc cheered, as he rubbed his hands together. "Now it's getting interesting. Think hard about what you want the ladies to do for you, Liam."

"I'm *already* hard," Liam said.

I looked through the table top between his legs and saw his good-sized cock pointing straight up on his belly.

Marc reached into his tray and tossed another black marker on the table. Heather paused trying to read his face, then she glanced beneath the table at his throbbing cock.

"I think he's bluffing," she said. "I'll match your bet and raise you one hundred." She threw down her last two black chips then dealt the last card face up. She got another ten and Liam got a six.

Liam didn't hesitate to throw his last black chip in the pot.

"I call," he said, then he turned over his hole card and revealed three Kings.

"Whoa," Heather said, opening her eyes wide in surprise. She turned over her card and revealed a two. Liam had won the hand.

"Well played, young man," Heather said. "Your wish is our command. What would you like us to do?"

Liam ran his eyes up and down Heather's figure and smiled.

"I want you to spread your legs and play with yourself."

Heather pushed her chair back from the table to give everyone a commanding view of her crotch, then she spread her legs apart. She began to circle her clit, while she stared Liam directly in the eyes. His breathing increased as his gaze wandered between her legs. She began to move her hips on the chair, and Liam's hand dropped down to his lap where he began rubbing his cock.

"Hey!" Heather admonished. "That's not allowed. You get to watch only."

"But you said as long as we don't cum—"

"There'll be plenty of time for that later. I want you boys to save those nice big hard-ons for the main event."

Heather sat back up and handed the remaining pack of cards to Liam.

"Your turn to deal," she said.

"That's it?" Liam said. "That was hardly worth three hundred dinars!"

Heather placed her moist fingers in her mouth and licked off her juices.

"You better play your hand wisely the rest of the way, then. Now you've got some extra cash to up the ante. We're just getting started."

Liam collected the pot from the middle of the table, then we all threw in two blue chips for the next round. Liam dealt the cards, and I won the next round with a full house.

I looked at Marc and Liam and licked my lips. I noticed that Liam's dick had lost some of its firmness, but Marc's was rapidly elongating under the table. I wondered how far he'd be willing to go with this game.

"I want Liam to suck Marc's cock," I said.

"What?" Liam said, his eyes flying open. "But I'm not...*gay*."

"It's just a game," Heather said. "No one's going to cum in your mouth, right Marc? At least not yet. Besides, how do you know if you don't like it until you try? Now get down there and suck that bratwurst."

Marc swung his chair out, and I noticed his cock was standing at full mast. Apparently at least *one* of the boys liked the idea of sucking another guy. Liam walked around the table and kneeled down in front of Marc. He stared at the tip of Marc's manhood, unsure what to do.

"Go on," Heather said. "It won't bite you. Just think of it as a popsicle. A very large warm popsicle."

Marc pulled his arms around behind his chair and clasped his hands together to give Liam freer access.

Liam opened his mouth and slowly lowered himself over the head of Marc's joystick. At first he just held it there, but after a few seconds he began to bob his head as Marc slowly swung his hips. They both seemed to be enjoying it, and I had to fight hard to keep my hands away from my steaming pussy. The sight of seeing two hetero men going at it was incredibly erotic. I wanted to see if I could push it a little further.

"Now play with his balls," I ordered.

Liam paused and peered up at me out of the corner of his eyes, and I simply nodded. Marc pushed his hips toward the end of his seat until his tight balls poked over the edge. Liam reached up and cupped them then rolled them gently between his fingers. His own cock had resumed its full length and was bobbing against his flat stomach. It was obvious that he was getting turned on by the experience, and I saw his tongue begin to roll around in his mouth as he circled the head of Marc's cock. Marc let out a groan and lifted his hips higher. I would have happily forfeited the game at that moment to watch Marc cum in Liam's mouth, but Heather interjected to remind us of the rules.

"Okay, I think that's enough for this round," she said. "You boys seem to be having a little bit too much fun."

Liam sheepishly disengaged from Marc and returned to his seat at the other side of the table. We resumed the game, with each round ratcheted up the degree of engagement between the players. Marc won the next round and asked Heather to sit in my lap while we tribbed each other for a couple of minutes. Then Heather won the next round and asked the men to do the same as we watched them jack their two cocks together between their bellies. By the time our hour was up, all four of us were worked up enough to jump each other bones. When we counted our chips, Heather had eked out Liam for the largest residual.

"What now?" Liam said, his cock bobbing on his stomach, already leaking pre-cum.

"I ended up with the highest winnings," Heather said, "so I get to decide on the final group activity. And I think we should all come back to my cabin."

We didn't bother to clean up the table as we quickly found the nearest exit. Unlike our first night together when we'd scurried down the stairs to her stateroom, this time we took the elevator down the three levels to her floor. But the tension in the lift was palpable as none of us said a word to one another, holding our collective breath in anticipation of what would come next.

9

FOUR PLAY

When we got to Heather's room, nobody was sure who should make the first move. When it was just the three of us, Heather hadn't hesitated to jump the only man in the room, but this time we had to figure out what to do with Liam. The obvious thing would have been for us to pair up as two hetero couples, but Heather had seen enough in the games room to have other ideas.

"You boys lie down on the bed with your feet facing each other," she ordered.

Marc and Liam dutifully lay on the mattress as Heather instructed.

"Now bend your knees and move together until your cock and balls are touching one another."

I looked at Heather inquisitively, wondering what she had planned. We'd already seen the men frotting their cocks together in the games room, and I was eager for some of my own touching.

She glanced at Marc and Liam's glistening cocks throbbing against each other and smiled at me.

"Do you want to go first or me?"

I pinched my eyebrows for a second, then gasped when I understood her intention. The idea of having two cocks inside me was something I hadn't yet experienced. I moved toward the bed and kneeled on the mattress straddling the two men, facing Liam. I'd already watched Marc come inside me, this time I wanted to picture a younger man's reaction.

The men paused for a moment, unsure what I wanted. They were probably thinking of the classic DP maneuver, where one would fuck me in my pussy while the other fucked me up the ass. But I had a better idea. Ever since I saw them rubbing their cocks together in the game room, I'd fantasized about grasping them both inside my pussy. Both men were well hung, measuring together at least three times the girth of an average man's erect penis, but I figured if my anatomy could accommodate a baby's head during childbirth, surely it could take the equivalent of two good sized English cucumbers.

I reached around behind my ass and clasped their two penises together then slowly lowered my pussy until it touched the wet heads of their joined hard-ons. Marc's was a little bit longer, so it pushed its way through first, as I felt my lips widen to accommodate his large organ. Slowly sitting down another inch, I could feel Liam's cockhead pressing me apart still further, and I moaned as I felt my pussy stretch to take them both inside me. With both of them lying flat on their backs on the mattress, there was little they could do with the full weight of my body pressing down over their hips. I relished the feeling of control, watching Liam's face contorting in pleasure as my love tunnel squeezed over their joined cocks.

I slowly lowered myself until I felt my vulva resting on Liam's stubbly pubis. I was glad I'd placed Marc in the posterior position, where he had a little more room to sheath his larger cock. I began to use my thigh muscles to move up and down over their connected meat and reflected back on the Asian girl's two-headed cock from the view room the previous day. Two double pricks in as many days was a new milestone for me.

It seemed as if every nook and crevice of my pussy was filled up by the hot, throbbing manhood of these two virile men. I humped them faster, knowing it wouldn't to take long for all of us to come after the long buildup in the game room. Before long, Heather decided she wanted a piece of the action, and I could hear Marc's muffled moans behind me as she sat over his face. The look on Liam's face was priceless. I wasn't sure which he was enjoying more—the feeling of having his cock deeply embedded in my wet pussy, or the feeling of having Marc's throbbing member next to his.

His mouth was wide open as he moaned loudly in pleasure, and I knew he wouldn't be long to this world. I placed my hands over his tight pecs and squeezed the two-headed python inside me as I felt a powerful urge welling inside me. Heather suddenly reached around my back and squeezed my tits and we all howled in unison. When I came, I bucked wildly over the two men as I felt their cocks pulsing together, flooding me inside with their honey.

I sat there for a minute savoring the feeling of having two hard dicks inside me, as I peered out Heather's balcony window at the sun setting over the ocean. This cruise had been one hell of an adventure, and I didn't know if or when I'd have another chance like this again. I wanted to make it last as long as possible.

VOLUME THREE

PEEP SHOW

1

———

After going over a week without any type of intimate contact, I was feeling especially horny today. In such circumstances, I'd normally go online to find an outlet to relieve my built-up sexual tension. But lately, I'd been finding that internet porn wasn't doing it for me. Sure, the girls were always hot and sexy and I could generally find something new and interesting to get me in the mood. But it all seemed so impersonal, so *manufactured*. Even my favorite lesbian webcam site had become a disappointment, with viewers swiping from one partner to the next, often right in the middle of a hot-and-heavy session.

I needed some real flesh and blood contact, or at least be able to *see* someone live. But I didn't just want to see and hear her, I wanted to smell her, feel her, *taste* her. Somebody who wouldn't exit the scene at the first sign of boredom, or as soon as she got her rocks off. I wanted to be with someone I could take my time with and enjoy the experience on my own terms. And *Tinder* was out of the question, since I didn't have the time or the energy to vet the candidates, nor string along the ones whose profile never seemed to align with their real personas.

After trolling through the usual online sources, I decided to try something new. I clicked on the latest issue of the Windy City Times, Chicago's long-time LGBTQ newspaper. At least here, I knew I knew I'd be able to find authentic lesbian, bi, and trans girls. Among the litany of gay bar postings, I found an unusual listing in the classified section. Under the headline *Nude Casting Call* was an ad for open auditions at the local theater company. Intrigued, I clicked on the Details tab and began to read the full description:

> *The Bijou Theater is looking for uninhibited people who are interested in staging solo performances in the nude. With a king-size bed as your primary prop, your goal is to arouse and titillate a live audience using only your body and your wild imagination. There will be boys-only, girls-only, and mixed couples events, so you can cater your performance to your own sexual preference or mix it up as you see fit.*
>
> *A winner will be chosen after each audition based on audience response, with the winners moving on to regional semi-finals and finals. The Grand Prize winner will win an all-expense-paid vacation for two to the Desire Riviera Maya Resort in Puerto Morales, Mexico. Exhibitionists and voyeurs alike are encouraged to attend. Come one, come all!*

Holy shit, I thought, suddenly aware of the growing dampness in my panties. The idea of watching someone perform an erotic routine for a live audience definitely got my motor running. This wasn't some sleazy dive bar or strip club where the girls performed nude dances in front of a bunch of leering men. This was a legitimate theater where amateur performers volunteered to display their naked bodies to a group of of anonymous strangers in a darkened auditorium. And I could *choose* the target audience–no sweaty old men, no creepy lap dances, no private rooms where the girls were paid for private favors. I could just sit back and enjoy the show in the privacy of my own darkened alcove.

But what exactly did they mean by *solo performances*? Just how far did these performances go? Did they touch their bodies only superfi-cially, simulating sex acts like a typical stripper? Or did they caress themselves in their most private regions, with the purpose of genuinely getting themselves and their onlookers off? The presence of a bed on the stage suggested it would be more than just a typical erotic dance. And how much audience participation would there be in the production? Were spectators allowed to actively stimulate *themselves* in the dark while they watched the performers on stage?

The more I thought about it, the more turned on I got imagining how exciting it would be to take in a live performance. Hell, if the conditions were right and the security was good enough, I might be tempted to give it a go myself. But first, I needed to check it out from the protection of the viewing gallery. At least there I'd be able to get my rocks off watching somebody else in the relative safety of a darkened auditorium. We could *both* take our time to ramp up our desire, knowing the only consideration was maximizing everyone's viewing pleasure and satisfaction.

I clicked on the Calendar tab and noticed a selection of dates highlighted in different colors and markings. Pink shading signified ladies-only nights, blue was men-only, and green was open to both sexes. A downward-sloping diagonal line through the box meant the show was sold out for new audience members, and an upward-sloping line meant auditions had been fully booked for that day's event. Scrolling through the pink-shaded boxes, I saw that the next three week's events were X'd out, indicating there was no room for either performers or attendees. The next available ladies night only had one line crossed through it, so I click on the date and booked a ticket immediately.

As I leaned back in my chair, imagining myself watching a pretty girl caressing herself on stage, I pulled down my panties and began rubbing my inflamed clit.

This is going to be interesting, I thought.

When the audition night finally arrived, I went to the theater and presented my online ticket to the attendant. A few other girls were waiting along with me behind the turnstiles, and after security checked our driver's licenses to verify our age and sex, they handed each of us a small bag and we entered the darkened theater, locating the closest seats to the stage. I peered in the bag and saw that it contained two items: a disposable plastic seat cover and a small box of Kleenex tissues. I smiled knowingly, then carefully spread the latex cover over the top of my chair. When I sat down and peered around me, I noticed that the room was only half full. Most of the seats were occupied by lone viewers with at least two or three open spaces separating them. I nodded, happy with the way the theater had set everything up for the maximum privacy and comfort of the spectators.

But I noticed there was also a sprinkling of same-sex couples strewn about the theater who were giggling and making out in their private cubbyholes. There was just enough light to notice that everybody was female, but not enough to establish their identities. Suddenly, the lights dimmed and a middle-aged woman walked out onto the middle of the stage under a bright spotlight. I recognized a familiar shape in the shadows behind her, and my heart began to flutter knowing that a nude performer would soon be lying on the bed, giving us a show to remember.

"Good evening, *ladies and voyeurs!*" she announced, holding the mic to her mouth. "Are you ready for some uniquely stimulating entertainment?"

A few people whooped and hollered, while others clapped excitedly. I wondered how many in the audience were 'regulars' who were there mostly to pass judgement on the performances, versus the first-timers like me who were there mostly for the intrigue and the stimulation.

"Those of you who've been here before already know the rules," the woman continued. "But allow me to educate the rest of the crowd to ensure the safety and satisfaction of all participants."

The buzz in the theater suddenly subsided as everyone allowed the MC to finish her briefing.

"Audience members are permitted to encourage the performers with verbal feedback, but we ask that you keep it upbeat at all times. Many of our performers are first-time auditioners, and we wish to provide them with a positive environment to express themselves openly. At the end of each performance we'll ask for your collective feedback to help us judge who should be moved on to the next stage of the competition. No booing or cat-calls–only clapping or cheering to reflect the degree to which you felt entertained. As always, we ask you to remain in your seats until the end of each performance unless you need to use the restrooms in the rear of the theater. For the safety and privacy of every performer, no one will be permitted to approach the stage at any time. Anyone breaking these rules will be promptly escorted out of the theater."

The woman paused for a moment to make sure everyone understood the ground rules. I nodded my head, beginning to appreciate the level of safety and security afforded the performers and audience members alike.

"Any questions?" the MC asked.

The room filled with silence, as everybody anticipated the next move.

"All right then," she said, swinging her arm to the side of the stage where the spotlight focused on a closed curtain hanging in the wings. "Let the show begin!"

As she receded to the opposite side of the stage, the curtain parted and a young woman looking to be in her late teens or early twenties tiptoed out onto the stage wearing a thin bathrobe. She glanced shyly toward the darkened auditorium, then walked purposefully across the stage to the king-size bed, now brightly illuminated under two criss-crossing spotlights. When she reached the edge of the bed, she paused for a moment then pulled her robe off her body and hung it on the side of the headboard, quickly slipping under the linen sheets.

I was able to catch just enough of her naked body to see that she had a petite frame and an agile figure. Her ass was firm and round, and her legs tapered with the grace of a short-track sprinter. I wondered if she might have been a college athlete. Because she'd turned her body away from the audience as she got under the covers, I wasn't able to see much of her upper body, which she'd kept carefully covered with crossed arms. But her face was young and pretty, with the plump skin, full eyebrows, and the unruffled hairstyle of a carefree adolescent.

My pussy twitched as I watched her climb into the bed, pulling the sheets high up under her neck with two hands. I smiled at how shy she was and wondered what had prompted her to participate in such an event if she felt so nervous about displaying her body. Maybe it had been a dare between her and her friends, or maybe her boy or girlfriend had put her up to it, or maybe she just wanted to experience the excitement of being naked in a room full of strangers. Either way, I found the whole premise highly stimulating, and I squirmed in my seat as I found myself getting more turned on by the moment.

I'd decided to wear a mid-length skirt and button-up blouse with no underwear underneath to provide maximum freedom of movement in the event I had the opportunity to touch myself. As I watched the girl lower one hand down the front of her abdomen under the thin sheet, my legs began to spread apart unconsciously. She still held the covers tightly under her chin with one hand, but the flimsy fabric meandering like a snake left little doubt what she was doing. At first, she teasingly cupped one of her breasts with her free hand, pinching the nipple with her fingers as her eyes darted tentatively around the darkened theater. I could tell she was nervous and excited at the same time, and I was happy she couldn't see any of our faces to embolden her actions.

Mmm, a few people in the audience hummed, encouraging her to continue. The girl smiled then inched her hand lower down her abdomen. When it reached the top of her hips, I saw her fingers probe the area near the base of her mound, and her face twitched when she found her sensitive spot. As she began to circle her fingers over her love button, my own fingers began to inch under my skirt toward my tingling gland. There was something incredibly sexy about watching a young girl touch herself under the covers, knowing that everyone's eyes in the room were glued on her.

With the murmurs from the audience turning from hums of approval to gentle moans, the girl slowly began to spread her legs, as the movement of her hand between her legs started to speed up. I could see her chest beginning to rise and fall as her desire began to mount, and she tried to keep a straight face as her lips puckered and her eyelashes batted intermittently while a gentle flush began to spread over her cheeks.

"Show us more!" one of the couples in the corner yelled.

The girl stopped moving for a moment, temporarily taken aback by the intrusion, then she slowly lowered the cover down to the base of her hips. Her tits were small but perky, resting high on her chest in a sexy crescent shape, with large areolas and dark nubs. She lifted her other hand from under the sheet and cupped both of them, pinching her hardening nipples between her fingers.

"*Yes,*" somebody purred a few rows in front of me.

Emboldened by the audience's reaction, the girl soon traced one hand back down under the sheets and resumed stimulating her pussy. As I watched the sheets tenting and puffing from the action of her hand, I slipped my own hand under my skirt and began mimicking her movement, stroking and caressing my little man-in-the-boat. I didn't know exactly why, but I found the experience of watching a live girl touching herself in a darkened theater much more arousing than watching somebody masturbate online.

I was dying to see more of her body and just when I was about to encourage her to pull the sheets down a little further, someone else in the audience beat me to it.

"Let us see your pretty pussy," someone called from the back of the theater.

The girl paused for a moment, unsure how much she wanted to reveal. Then she drew her legs back together and pulled the covers down over her knees. I could see her hairy muff sitting on top of her mound, glistening from the juices she'd been spreading over the area with her free hand. She began to separate her legs, then suddenly stopped, not ready to reveal her most private areas to a room full of strangers. But her heaving chest indicated that she was still turned on and desperate to touch herself.

Suddenly, she flipped over onto her stomach, placing both of her hands under her crotch with her legs tightly closed. As I watched her buttocks flexing and her hips pressing rhythmically down onto the mattress, it became apparent to everyone watching exactly what she was doing with her hands. While her hips began to flop up and down on the mattress, her mouth spread open as a flush rolled over her face.

Fuck, I murmured to myself, watching her jill herself under her stomach. *That is so hot!*

Seeing her masturbating so demurely with her pretty ass and back toward us was somehow even more of a turn-on than watching her close-up. I thrust my fingers inside my cunt and began fucking myself more vigorously, imagining myself straddling her with a strap-on dildo.

God, how I'd like a piece of that pretty ass.

"Spread your legs further apart!" someone called from the other side of the theater.

As if on cue, the girl began to spread her thighs until they were separated about thirty degrees apart. I could now see her fingers moving rapidly between her cleft with the underside of her glistening slit poking tantalizingly between her pink globes.

As the sound of impassioned sighs and moans began to spread around the theater, I glanced around me and noticed the telltale sign of movement in the adjacent seats. Many of the girls in my row had their legs spread wide apart as they stroked their pussies while they watched the pretty girl on the stage grow increasingly excited. I glanced at one of the couples in the corner and saw that one girl had her leg raised over the armrest while her partner rammed her fingers into her snatch as she kissed her passionately.

Suddenly, the girl on the stage began to moan more loudly as she angled her ass upwards, spreading her knees further apart. We could now see her entire glistening vulva, highlighted by the twin spotlights shining on her ass, from her pretty pink pucker down past her slit all the way to her hairy muff. As she sped up the movement of her right hand circling her clit, she reached further down between her legs with her other hand and inserted two fingers inside her hole.

She was now unashamedly fucking herself with two hands for the entire theater to see, with no further impediments, or hint of shyness. I could hear the sound of other fingers sloshing in and out of pussies all around me as other horny audience members rammed themselves in sympathy with the girl on the stage. Within seconds, a crimson flush spread over the girl's cheeks and her buttocks began to tremble. As her knees began to wobble from side to side, she squealed like an injured animal, caught up in the throes of a powerful orgasm.

Watching her come in full view of the surrounding audience was more than I could bear, and I arched my back, clamping down hard over my fingers, spraying my pent-up juices all over the metal back of the seat in front of me. As soft gasps and groans emanated from every corner of the theater, the turned-on crowd released their own pent-up pleasure in tandem with the pretty co-ed. I glanced over at the lesbian couple in the corner and saw the girl with her leg over the armrest convulsing in pleasure as her partner rammed her fist into her while they both watched the stage, transfixed by the erotic performance.

When the pretty coed finally stopped shaking, she pulled the sheets back up over her body and the stage darkened, as the spotlight shifted to the curtains on the opposite side of the rostrum. The MC walked back out onto the platform, holding a small device in her hand.

"What did you guys think?" she asked, pointing her smartphone out to the crowd. "Was that worthy of an encore appearance?"

"Woo-hoo!" some audience members hollered.

I noticed a needle swing clockwise on the decibel-reading app.

"Let's give the young lady a *proper* round of applause," the MC hollered. "Show her how much you all *really* enjoyed the performance!"

The crowd erupted in applause and cheering, demonstrating their appreciation and satisfaction with the performance. I noticed the needle swing about sixty percent of the way around the circle, and the MC turned the device around to register the results.

"Let's take a little breather while we give our next performer a few minutes to prepare," she nodded. "But compose yourselves, because the next performer is a crowd favorite!"

As the woman strolled back into the shadows, a group of stage-hands began remaking the now empty bed with a fresh set of linens.

I wish they'd offer us a similar turndown service, I thought as I wiped the back of the seat in front of me with one of the napkins provided in my care package. *Because if that girl only justifies a rating of sixty percent, I'm going to need some fresh towels before this evening is over.*

2

———————

As I watched the next three performers, I grew increasing aroused by the sexually charged atmosphere in the room. At the end of the evening, the prize for best performance was awarded to an older, more seasoned actor, but I couldn't get the image of the young coed shaking quietly on the bed out of my head. There was something about her self-effacing nature that turned me on like no one I'd seen in a long time. I went home that night and had three more powerful orgasms imagining it was *me* planted between her thighs instead of her hand.

But I had far from satisfied my thirst for this intoxicating production. I immediately booked the next available ladies-night audition then spent the next two weeks practicing my own erotic act in front of my full-length dressing mirror. I wasn't quite ready to go on stage and bare my soul for a room full of strangers, but I found the idea incredibly stimulating, and every time I thought about it I came harder than I had in a long time.

When the night of the next auditions rolled around, I was already soaking wet by the time I entered the building's lobby. I looked around me and saw a familiar collection of singles and couples waiting to be admitted, but there was one pretty girl at the end of the line who caught my eye. Wearing black tights and a loose-fitting, cropped t-shirt, her tight ass and plump breasts barely concealed by her open midriff got me even more excited. As I stole glances at her sexy body, dribbles of lubrication began streaming down the inside of my thighs under my pantyless skirt.

Everybody seemed too nervous to strike up a conversation while we waited to go inside, embarrassed by the obvious reason for our attendance at the event. Like a bunch of perverts in a peep-show theater, we just wanted to hide in the shadows while we silently got our rocks off watching the action on the stage. I turned my body sideways, trying to distract the girl's attention from the river cascading down my legs while pretending to fish around for something in my purse.

After presenting my ID to the security guard, I hurried through the turnstiles and walked into the darkened theater. It was more full than last time, but I found a secluded seat about fifteen rows back from the stage. As the lights began to dim in preparation for the main event, another viewer side-stepped her way into my row and stopped a few seats away from me. I looked up and noticed that it was the girl from the lobby.

"Is this spot taken?" she asked, pointing to the seat next to mine.

I glanced around the theater noticing a few other open spots slightly further back, but for some reason I didn't mind having my personal space encroached upon this time.

"Um, no," I said, motioning to the open seat. "Help yourself."

The girl opened her care package and spread the disposable seat cover over the chair then sat down, placing her purse on the opposite armrest. It felt a bit uncomfortable having someone sitting so close to me, but my rapidly beating heart belied my true feelings.

"It's a little busier than usual tonight," she said, spreading her legs apart to make herself more comfortable.

I glanced down between her thighs and noticed a dark patch in the crotch of her tight pants. Apparently more than one of us had gotten herself worked up in preparation for the night's festivities.

"Oh?" I said, pretending to be disinterested. "I wouldn't know–it's only my second time coming to this event."

"This must be my seventh or eighth time at least" she said, not letting me off the hook so easily. "When were you last here?"

"Two weeks ago, on the last ladies' night."

"I remember that one," she nodded. "That was the one with the cute college girl who needed a little extra encouragement to show her body."

"Yes."

"She was a hot little thing, wasn't she? But I thought she got cheated out the most erotic performance of the night. I guess the more skin they show and the more outrageous the performance, the higher the scores they receive from the hardcore regulars."

"Mmm," I nodded.

"Do you prefer girls?" she asked. "I mean to *watch*?"

"I guess so," I said. "I find them sexier, but I also feel safer around other women. I don't really want to be surrounded by a bunch of lecherous dudes jerking off a few feet away from me."

"I know what you mean," she said, lifting her sneakers off the floor, one at a time. "At least the theater keeps the place pretty clean. They probably have to send a hazmat team in here after each show."

I shuffled my ass on the latex seat beneath me and smiled.

"Thank heavens for these sanitary seat covers," I said. "I can't imagine sitting anywhere in this place without them."

"And the *napkins*," the girl said, waving one in front of her crotch. "You can never have enough of these things once the action gets hot and heavy."

I was about to introduce myself when the lights in the theater dimmed and the MC walked out onto the stage. But I hardly heard anything she said while I ogled the girl's body next to me. As she leaned back in her seat to get more comfortable, her cutoff shirt slid further up her abdomen, showing the bottom of her fleshy tits. The sensuous curve of her mounds taunted me in the shadows, and I squeezed my thighs together trying to quell my itchy clit.

When I looked back up toward the stage, a sexy blonde girl was kneeling on the bed facing the crowd with her thighs spread about two feet apart. She was wearing a full-length body suit with holes cut out over the tops of her breasts and crotch to reveal her private parts. The effect magnified the size of her breasts, highlighting her pink nipples poking sensuously out of the thin fabric. But it was the effect on her *lower* body than really got my juices flowing. The only part of her crotch that was showing was her bright pink vulva, shining like the petals of a flower surrounded by the darkened landscape of her tight-fitting leotard.

"*Fuck*, that's hot," the girl next to me hissed, spreading her legs wider apart.

The girl on the stage suddenly swung around with her back to the audience, straightening her legs to her sides as she slowly lowered her crotch to the surface of the bed, performing a perfect split. Then she tilted her ass slightly upward, revealing her pink slit shining like a conch shell on a barren beach. As I squirmed in my chair, mesmerized by the girl's erotic performance, my legs began to spread apart with a mind of their own.

"Do you mind if I make myself more comfortable?" the girl sitting next to me said, pulling her black tights down over her knees. "I'm feeling the need to give my pussy a little breathing room of its own."

"By all means," I said, now fully on board with the idea of having a partner I could enjoy the show with.

She pulled her tights down over her ankles, draping them over the back of the seat next to her, then placed her ankles on the seat rests in front of her, bending her knees as she tilted her hips forward. I could see her bald mound and protruding nub glistening in the reflected light from the stage as my own pussy began to dribble onto the seat cushion beneath me.

Some movement on the stage caught my attention, and I looked up to see the blond girl flip over like a breakdancer, slicing her legs open into a wide scissor shape. With one foot pointed tantalizingly toward the audience and the other nestled under her shoulder, she was practically *begging* us touch her glistening gash.

"*Damn*," my seatmate groaned, now unashamedly rubbing her

snatch with her right hand. "I'd sit on that pretty pussy and grind my cunt against hers *any* time."

I slid my hand under my skirt and began to circle my burning nub, thinking exactly the same thing. It had been a while since I'd felt another woman's wet pussy against my own, and I fantasized about kneeling between the blond girl's legs and lowering my hips onto hers.

"Mmm," I nodded as my body began to radiate in pleasure.

Hearing the sound of soft moans and sighs emanating from the amphitheater, the girl suddenly pulled her legs together and pointed them straight up in the air. The curl of her feet and the gentle musculature of her thighs as she flexed her legs reminded me of a ballerina, and I wondered if she might be a professional dancer. But it was the exposed folds of flesh between her tight buttocks that I was focused on at this particular moment. As they spilled out of her torn bodysuit like an open clam shell, my mouth watered imagining myself sucking her pretty pussy while she went through her poses.

Just when I thought it couldn't get any hotter, she lowered her legs into another perfect split framing her face as she peered out into the audience. She began to curl her body forward as she smiled at her hidden admirers while she rolled her fingers over her puffy petals.

"Fuck, yes," the girl next to me hissed, spreading her legs further apart until her knee touched my elbow resting beside her on my armrest. "That is one gorgeous pussy. I'd water that flower any day."

As my seatmate tilted her head back onto the backrest and sped up the motion of her hand between her pussy, the girl on the stage reached under the covers and lifted a strange-looking device into the air above her splayed body. It looked like a type of dildo, but not like anything I'd seen before. This one had deep diagonal grooves in the shaft, making it look like an oversize plastic screw. She tapped a button on the base of the unit it suddenly began to gyrate in a circular flapping motion. Then she held the tip against the opening of her pink slit and slowly sunk the rotating dildo into her hole.

While the crowd watched in mesmerized silence, she began to

shake her hips back and forth as she grasped her ankles with outstretched arms. The whole scene looked surreal–like she was some kind of bendable doll with an animatronic dildo flopping around in her snatch as she smiled out into the audience. But the flush spreading across her face quickly reminded me this was no act, as her mouth began to gape open from the pleasure that was spreading inside her body.

Suddenly the girl next to me turned to look for something in her purse and she pulled out a large dildo. I recognized the shape of it instantly, with its penis-shaped tip and protruding rabbit ears on the shaft. She tapped two buttons on the base, then plunged it deep inside her sopping pussy, ramming it in and out of her sloshing hole. Having one just like it at home, I knew exactly what was happening as she held it tightly against her with two hands. While circulating beads around the perimeter of the shaft stimulated the walls of her tunnel, the articulated tip rotated around in circles caressing her G-spot as the flapping external appendages straddled the shaft of her clit, providing intense external stimulation.

As I peered back and forth between the contortionist on the stage and the sexy girl ramming her pussy next to me, I plunged the fingers of my right hand into my hole and began groaning along with the rest of the audience. When the girl on the stage arched her back off the surface of the bed, bringing her face closer to the gyrating instrument flapping wildly inside her pussy, I could feel my own pleasure rising toward its inevitable denouement as my body began to tense up.

Suddenly, her buttocks and thighs began shaking as her head jerked forward and back in unison with the writhing serpent between her legs. I saw her sex flush spread up her long slender neck then all over her face as she grimaced in climactic pleasure.

"Oh my *God*," the girl next to me groaned as her own body began shaking in convulsive spasms with the pulsing vibrator buzzing between her legs. Seeing both girls coming so strongly soon put me over the edge as I slipped my knuckles past the opening to my pussy while I pounded my G-spot with my fist, grunting in a series of powerful contractions.

"Uhn, uhn, uhn," I groaned, feeling the pressure building inside my tunnel.

Just before I finished coming, I pulled my hand out of my hole, jetting my juices forward like a garden hose. The intense spray bounced off the back of the chair in front of me, sprinkling droplets all over the front of my seatmate's body. She looked up at me and mouthed the words *fuck me*, taken aback in surprise. I leaned over and kissed her passionately, cupping her quivering tits as she pressed the still-vibrating dildo hard against her vulva. When we both finally stopped coming, we flopped back against our seat rests, panting in exhaustion from the intense workout we'd both experienced watching the sexy scene on the stage.

3

———————

"Holy shit!" the girl next to me sighed when she finally came down from her intense climax. "That was *insane*. I've never seen anything like that before, and I've been to a lot of these performances. Whatever that thing was that was gyrating in her pussy, I want one of those."

"I know what you mean," I said. "I've got a pretty extensive collection of sex toys at home, but I've never seen anything like that before. Watching her use it hands-free with her legs spread apart was incredibly erotic."

As the brightly illuminated bed and the sexy blonde girl receded into the shadows, the MC walked back onto the stage.

"Did you enjoy that performance?" she asked.

"Woo-hoo!" the audience roared in unison.

"Hold up a sec," the MC said, removing her decibel-monitoring app from of her pocket and tapping the screen.

"Now tell me what you *really* think!" she said, turning the device toward the crowd.

Everybody hollered at the top of their lungs, clapping enthusiastically. The needle swung ninety percent of the way around the arc before stopping near the end of the red zone.

"That's going to be pretty hard to beat," the girl sitting next to me smiled.

She turned and extended her hand over the armrest between us.

"My name's Ashley. I suppose we should introduce ourselves now that we've gotten to know each other a little better."

"Jade," I said, clasping her hand with my wet fingers. "Sorry about the mess–I guess I got a little carried away by that last performance."

"That makes two of us," Ashley said, removing some napkins from her gift bag and handing me a few tissues. "I think you need these more than I do," she said, wiping my juice off the front of her face. "I've never seen a girl squirt as much as you do. You should consider putting on a performance of your own. With your special powers, you'd have a shot at going all the way."

I nodded my head as I cleaned the back of the chair in front of me.

"It's crossed my mind a couple of times. I could sure use a free trip to the tropics. But I'm not sure I've got the nerve to take off all my clothes in front of a group of strangers. I'm enjoying things plenty enough from right here in the viewing gallery."

I watched Ashley remove the dripping dildo from her pussy and wipe it off with a napkin. "What about you? You put on a pretty erotic show yourself. With your hot body, I'm sure you'd get some very appreciative scores of your own."

"I've thought about it," she said. "I guess I just haven't found a strong enough reason to give it a try yet. I'm still thinking of ideas for what I could do that would be new and different."

After the stagehands finished remaking the bed, the MC returned to the stage to introduce the next act.

"That last performance received one of the highest scores in a long time," she said. "But if anyone can top her, I'm guessing this next act has one of the best shots. Prepare yourselves for *Sappho and Aphrodite!*"

The curtain at the side of the stage parted and two naked redheads emerged, walking hand-in-hand toward the bed in the center of the stage. They looked remarkably alike, with similar builds, height, and the same auburn ringlets falling gently over their shoulders. I wondered if they might be twins, and I turned toward Ashley, pinching my eyebrows in surprise.

"I didn't know they allowed tandem acts," I said.

"It happens every now and then," she nodded. "But most people prefer to go solo. It's hard to judge a tandem act in terms of who should move forward to the next round. Sometimes, the MC asks the crowd to rate each performer separately, but in this case these girls almost look like *clones* of one another. It would be impossible to differentiate the two when it comes time to evaluate their performance."

"Do you think they're *sisters*?" I said.

"I dunno, but if they are, that's just notched it up a couple of levels in my books. Let's see how far they take it."

As I ogled the figures of the two girls walking across the stage, my pussy twitched imagining them touching one another. Their skin shone like alabaster under the bright light of the overhead spotlight, their pink nipples glowing like beacons on the pale canvas of their bodies. Their tits were very small, making them almost look like adolescent boys with their flat chests and narrow hips. But when they reached the side of the bed and climbed onto the mattress, their curvy asses and sexy slits left little doubt as to their real sex.

"Mmm," Ashley purred, placing her feet on the armrests in front of her, spreading her thighs apart. "There's nothing like fresh girl meat to get me in the mood. *Two* helpings are making me twice as hungry."

My own pussy pulsed imagining them growing up together, playing in the privacy of their own rooms. Whether they were real sisters or it was just part of their act, I'd already bought into the theme as my juices began to trickle down under my ass.

"They're fucking hot, that's for sure," I nodded, hiking my skirt up to reveal my glistening mound.

"Damn girl," Ashley grunted. "You look pretty edible yourself. I might need to take you home once the show is over to have you for dessert."

"That can be arranged," I purred, giving her a playful wink.

When we turned our attention back to the stage, the girls were lying down beside each other, rubbing their bodies together as they kissed passionately on the bed.

"Something tells me this isn't the *first* time they've been together this way," Ashley mused.

"No," I nodded, my eyes glued on the stage. "I have a feeling they've had quite a few years to prepare for this moment."

As they intertwined their legs and began to grind their mounds together, Ashley and I began to circle our tingling clits with our right hands.

"Mmm," I moaned. "I'd love to feel their sweet bodies pressed up against mine right about now."

"Do you need a little *assist*?" Ashley said, raising an eyebrow and reaching over the armrest to slip her fingers under my blouse.

"*Fuck*, yes," I hissed, dying to feel someone else's hands on my body.

I spread my legs far apart and rested the underside of my knees over the adjacent armrests like the couple I'd seen at the previous show. Ashley took one look at my pink nub poking its head out of its sheath and placed her other palm over my pussy, caressing my folds with the tips of her fingers.

"Yes, baby," I groaned. "Play with my clit while I watch these cute girls. I want to imagine I'm right there in the thick of the action."

"You like flat-chested girls, do you?" she purred, lifting her fingers to circle my burning jewel.

"Yes," I panted. "I reminds me of my adolescent years."

"Mmm," Ashley mewed. "The great taboo. It's off limits now that we're grown up, but I remember experimenting when I was younger too. I bet those two have been playing with each other for a long time."

"Yes," I groaned, beginning to lose myself in the fantasy.

The two redheads suddenly separated and shifted into a scissor position, lying on their sides as they reached out and clasped hands.

"*Fuck me*," I groaned, watching the two girls rubbing their pussies together.

"Does that turn you on?" Ashley purred, slipping her fingers inside me as she trilled my clit with her thumb.

"You have *no* idea," I purred.

"Oh, I've got a pretty good idea judging by how wet you are," she said. "Are you going to squirt all over their pretty little tits?"

"Fuck yes," I groaned, getting more and more worked up watching the two girls tribbing their wet pussies together.

"What exactly would you do with them if you had the opportunity?" Ashley asked. "What did you use to do with your girlfriends during sleepovers?"

"I'd touch them in their private areas," I panted. "Kiss them, suck them, *probe* them."

Ashley peered at me with a sly smile.

"Trib them, mount them, grind your pussies together?"

"Yes," I groaned, reflecting back on my earliest sexual discoveries.

"Did you squirt back then too?" she asked.

"Not right away. Not until I went through puberty and began lubricating more heavily."

"Did you cum with your little friends?"

"Yes," I said, beginning to tremble from the imagery of the two girls scissoring on the stage, reminding me of my explorative youth.

"What else did you like to do with your pretty girlfriends?" Ashley said, using the show on the stage as a metaphor for reliving my childhood memories.

"Sometimes we'd play with toys..." I said.

As if on cue, one of the girls lifted a long green object from under the covers, placing it between their pussies.

A cucumber! I murmured, remembering the moment when my girlfriends and I discovered how much fun it was to probe our pussies with whatever phallic-shaped objects we could find. As the girls separated their bodies, placing the ends of the cucumber against each of their openings, my juices began pouring over Ashley's hands.

"Do you want me to place my little toy inside you while you channel fucking these girls?" Ashley said.

"Yes, please," I begged, desperate to feel my pussy filled up while I imagined fucking the cute redheads.

Ashley reached over and lifted her rabbit vibrator off her seat cushion and without even bothering to turn it on, she rammed it inside my pussy, beginning to fuck me with the dildo as she leaned over to kiss me. I turned my face toward her and moaned into her mouth as I peered at the spectacle on the stage out of the corner of my eyes. The two girls now had the double-sided dildo deeply embedded in each of their pussies as they ground their vulvas together, moaning in unison. I could see their arms beginning to tense up as they held each other tightly, while their passion slowly built toward a peak.

Ashley tapped the base of the rabbit dildo, activating the dual vibration functions, and I slid down in my seat, pressing the flapping rabbit ears against my pussy.

"Oh *God*, Ashley," I panted. "I'm going to cum baby. I'm going to cum so *hard*..."

As I watched the pre-orgasmic rash begin to spread over the chests of the two pale-skinned girls writhing together on the bed, my pleasure suddenly crested and I groaned a deep guttural growl. As the redheads began convulsing and wailing in union, the walls of my pussy clenched in powerful convulsions and I sprayed my juices out my plugged hole, ricocheting off the top of the vibrator towards Ashley's face.

While I thrashed in my seat squealing in ecstasy, she smiled at me, blinking her eyes between the sprays bouncing off her face while she held the vibrating dildo firmly against my vulva. Suddenly I became aware of similar noises in the theater as other viewers groaned in unison with the two girls shaking on the bed. The action of the two youthful-looking girls had brought back a flood of fond memories and it took a long time for me to stop coming as I watched them pleasure each other on the stage. When I finally came down from my high and collapsed back against my seat, Ashley looked over at me and smiled.

"We've *got* to get together soon," she mewed, lifting her dripping hand to my breast and pinching my erect nipple.

"Let's get out of here," I said, thrusting my tongue into her mouth. "I can't wait a moment longer."

"What about the rest of the show?" Ashley said, motioning to the MC walking back out onto the stage.

"*Fuck* the rest of the show," I said. "Let's make our *own* show. I need to feel your body next to mine before I go crazy."

Ashley paused for a moment, then peered at me with a sly grin. She raised herself out of her chair and sat her naked ass down over my still-fluttering pussy.

"Why wait any longer?" she said, tilting her pussy towards mine as she rested her arms on the seat rest in front of us. "Maybe we can have it *both* ways."

As she began to rock her hips against mine, I felt our clits merge as a new surge of energy rocketed through me. I grabbed her ass with both hands and pulled her closer toward me.

"Fuck yes," I purred. "Let's show these guys how it's really done..."

4

———————

After the show, Ashley and I went back to my place and made love all night long. Both of us had ideas for what we'd like to do for our own auditions, and we experimented with different positions and pairings for many hours. By the time I fell asleep at three a.m., I dreamed of all the adventurous things we might try on stage. In the morning, I slipped on a robe and went downstairs to cook up some breakfast and Ashley followed soon after.

"Mmm–that smells good," Ashley said, smelling the bacon and eggs frying in the pan.

"I thought you might be hungry after our little workout last night," I winked.

"*Little*?" she said, raising her eyebrows. "Between the two of us, we must have burned enough calories to light a small city."

I handed her a steaming mug of coffee and sat down on the bar stool next to her.

"That was pretty wild, wasn't it?"

"Are you referring to the action on the stage or how quickly we landed in each other's laps?"

"Both," I smiled. "I don't think I've come so hard as when you were grinding your pussy against mine while we watched the show together in the darkness."

"Viewing a live sex act can be pretty damn stimulating ," Ashley nodded. "I think it's genius what they've created there. I didn't realize how much I enjoyed being a voyeur until I discovered this production. But I think I'm just about ready to flip things around."

"Oh?" I said, lifting the food out of the skillet and placing it on her plate. "You think you're daring enough to bare everything in front of a group of strangers?"

"They won't *all* be strangers," she smiled, caressing my arm with the back of her hand. "*You'll* be there, right? It'll be that much more of a turn-on knowing you'll be watching too."

She paused for a moment as she wolfed down another spoonful of scrambled eggs.

"But it'll be even *more* exciting if we do it together."

"You mean as a tandem act, or each of us separately?"

"Both. It will be exciting for us to perform solo, but we can step it up to the next level if we decide to get together. That way, at least *one* of us will have a chance to win the trip to Mexico."

"You're just hedging your bets in case I win it for myself," I said, crunching on a piece of bacon.

"Well, if we each perform solo, we double our chances. Will you be my plus-one if I win?"

"Or you can be *mine* when *I* win," I smiled.

"Then when we get together as a couple, we can wow the crowd all over again," Ashley said. "It can only *help*, right?"

"I think you might be onto something," I nodded, finishing the last of my breakfast. "But now I've worked up a whole different kind of appetite. Do you feel like going back upstairs and working on some of our routines?"

"I thought you'd never ask," Ashley said, sliding her last piece of bacon sensuously between her lips.

For the next couple of hours, Ashley and I bounced ideas back and forth as we play-acted our routines in front of one another, giving each other tips and encouragement for how we could ramp up the excitement level. Then we practiced every combination we could imagine for joining together while we watched ourselves in my dressing mirror. By the time we both fell asleep exhausted again, I felt I'd vastly improved my repertoire of girl-on-girl sex.

When the date for the next auditions rolled around, we tingled in excitement waiting in the wings for our turns to go on stage. The first performer was a pretty brunette dressed in a cowboy hat and pantless chaps. She carried a pommel-horse-shaped apparatus onto the stage, then placed it in the center of the bed and plugged it into the nearest power outlet. After screwing a diamond-shaped dildo into the middle of the saddle, she spent the next thirty minutes riding it like a bucking bronco, flailing her arms in the air as the plug vibrated inside her. By the time she'd finished riding it in the forward- and backward-cowgirl positions, Ashley and I estimated that she'd had least four orgasms.

The next performers were a tandem act, dressed in sexy super-hero costumes. The lower half of the Batgirl character's costume had been entirely cut away, with her naked ass and bare legs posing a sexy counterpoint to her well-camouflaged upper body covered with a black mask, tight rubber bodice, and flapping yellow cape. Her Catwoman sidekick had the front of her full-length bodysuit slit open down the front, pressing her large round breasts into a sexy cleavage exposed on the front of her chest. They'd had some additional props placed on the stage and the Catwoman character entered first, creeping furtively toward a nightstand at the side of the bed. She opened the drawer, peering nervously around her, then she tucked a jewelry box under her arm.

Suddenly, Batgirl entered from the other side of the stage and confronted the would-be burglar, placing her hands on her hips and shaking her head in disapproval. Catwoman pulled out a whip and snapped it toward her adversary, but the Batgirl used her quick reflexes to sidestep the rippling cord. Then she pulled a foam boomerang out of her utility belt and flung it at Catwoman, striking her in the head as she fell to the floor, pretending to be unconscious. She then carried the girl to the bed and tied her to the four bedposts using wrist ties from her utility belt, spreading her arms and legs in a wide V-shape.

It was only then that I noticed the crotch of Catwoman's tights had also been split open, revealing her pink vulva surrounded by the black bodysuit. As she woke up from her stupor and took stock of her predicament, she sneered at Batgirl, flailing her body helplessly against her binds. Batgirl simply smiled back at her and reached into her utility belt, pulling out a large penis-shaped vibrator. She flipped a button on the base and the dildo began buzzing and throbbing loudly. As Batgirl lowered it toward her captive's open crotch in a threatening gesture, Catwoman thrashed her body on the bed, pretending to be frightened.

The whole scene was over-the-top campy, but somehow the appearance of the two skimpily clad superheroes pretending to battle created a highly arousing effect. Ashley and I looked at one another shaking our heads in dismay, wondering the same thing.

"I didn't know we were allowed to wear *costumes* and use *props*," she said. "Do you think our act is going to be interesting enough after this performance?"

"Let's see what else they've got in their bag of tricks," I said. "Remember it's not about the size of your package, it's how well you can use it."

As we peered back out onto the stage, Batgirl placed the vibrating tip of the dildo against Catwoman's mound and she suddenly stopped flailing as she lifted her hips to press the device firmer against her vulva. Batgirl peered at her devilishly, then pulled the vibrator away from her pussy as Catwoman feigned frustration. Then she held it against her flapping thighs for a few more seconds before yanking it away once again. They continued this cat-and-mouse routine for a few minutes until Catwoman shook her body angrily, looking at Batgirl with pleading eyes.

Batgirl picked the jewelry case up off the floor and pointed toward it with a disapproving stare, then motioned toward the nightstand where it belonged. Catwoman nodded her head in acquiescence, then Batgirl placed the container back in the table and held the vibrator high up in the air for the audience to see. They cheered her loudly, encouraging her to place it back on Catwoman's twitching vulva. But this time she inserted the huge phallus into Catwoman's pussy until it was fully embedded inside her. Then she proceeded to pump it in and out of her hole as Catwoman became increasingly aroused, moaning and writhing on the mattress until she climaxed in a powerful orgasm. When they finished their routine, the audience roared in approval, clapping enthusiastically.

"That's gonna be pretty hard to beat," Ashley said, knowing it was her turn to go on next. "Maybe I should have dressed up in a costume or brought some extra props."

"Don't worry about what other people are doing," I assured her, squeezing her hand gently. "With your hot bod and your sexy routine, you'll have them eating out of your hands in no time."

"Or hopefully my *crotch*," she smiled at me nervously.

"Exactly," I said. "Go do your thing. Remember, I'll be here watching the whole time getting turned-on along with you."

"Mmm," Ashley purred. "That'll help. Maybe I won't need as much lube after all."

I smiled back at her, nudging her out the curtain, and she walked toward the newly remade bed with her hands resting in the side pockets of her robe. We'd both agreed that her act would be sexier if she revealed her body in stages, teasing the audience about what she intended to do on stage. When she reached the bed, she climbed up onto the mattress and straddled the brass headboard, placing one knee on the pillow and her other foot on the opposite rail for support.

She began rocking her hips sexily on the top rail and opened the front of her robe, showing her plump tits sitting high on her chest. As she slowly slid her body toward the corner bedpost, she peered up at me and I nodded, circling my hand over my crotch to signal how much her act was turning me on. When she reached the end of the rail, she grasped the small brass globe topping the post and rolled her hands over it like she was giving it a sexy hand job. But she and I both knew she was actually lubing the ball with some tissues she'd hidden in her pockets. Then she lifted herself up and straddled the post between her thighs, lowering herself down a few inches.

To the audience watching from an oblique angle, they couldn't have known immediately what she was doing, with her robe still covering half of her body. But for me watching directly in front of her, I could see that she'd embedded the brass finial deep inside her pussy. When she reached back and pulled her robe off her body, an audible gasp rose from the audience when they finally realized what she was doing. With appreciate applause wafting up from the seats, Ashley placed both of her hands on the top rail and began to rock her body up and down over the brass bulb. As it became obvious she was fucking the bedpost, many observers began to moan while they stimulated themselves watching her erotic act.

When she peered back over towards me, I was squeezing my right breast tightly while my other hand fluttered between my legs. I nodded at her quietly as my body began to tremble in concert with hers, losing myself in her performance. Even though we'd talked about what we planned to do once we were on stage, I hadn't realized how sexy it would be to watch her first hand with the audience buzzing around us.

As Ashley became increasingly aroused listening to the reaction of the audience, she turned her body to face them directly, spreading her knees wide apart so they could clearly see her impaled over the bedpost. Her movements began to pick up in intensity and her neck muscles started to tighten as she approached climax. Suddenly she lurched forward, jerking her body forward and back from the convulsions racking her body.

As I watched her shaking in the throes of agony, I came unconsciously watching my new friend pleasure herself in front of the large audience. After many long seconds of quivering in pleasure, she slowly lifted herself off the glistening pole and pulled her robe back over her body, scampering off the stage in my direction. As the lights fell over the platform, the audience cheered loudly in appreciation of her sexy and original performance.

5

———

"What did you think?" Ashley said, scurrying up next to me.

"That was fucking hot," I said, holding her tightly as I motioned toward the still-buzzing amphitheater. "And judging by the audience reaction, *they* enjoyed it too. How did it feel being on stage? Were you nervous at all?"

"A little at first," she nodded. "But once I got that ball inside me, I wasn't thinking of much else. Other than watching *you,* of course. Knowing you were getting turned on watching me was more exciting than knowing everybody else was watching me."

"I'm glad," I said. "Did you enjoy yourself?"

"You have no idea," she smiled. "Let's just say the turnaround crew might need a little longer to clean up the bed in preparation for the next act.

"Speaking of which," she said, slipping her hand inside my robe to cup my quivering breast. "Are you ready to go out there? You seem a bit nervous yourself."

"That's just me still feeling excited from watching you. I've never felt more ready to do something like this in my whole life."

"Break a leg, babe," Ashley smiled. "Just make sure you don't break anything *else*." She held up her hands as I turned around for her to help me disrobe. "Are you sure you want to go out there completely naked?"

"It'll just get in the way," I said. "I just want it to be my naked body they're focused on. Hopefully that'll be enough."

"You don't need any props or extra embellishments," Ashley said. "You'll be doing something nobody's ever seen before."

"Wish me luck then," I said, hearing the MC come back out onto the stage to introduce the next act.

"You won't need it," Ashley said. "I'll see you soon."

I smiled back at her, knowing it would be sooner than anybody expected.

As the MC motioned toward the stagehands, the curtain swung open and I strutted across the stage, relishing every step as the audience took in my taut, hourglass figure. I'd worked hard to keep my thirty-something body in good shape and as I extended my legs with each step, wiggling my ass and holding my chest high, my body surged with fire. I was about to do something I'd never tried before, and the idea of touching myself in front of a room full of strangers electrified me.

When I reached the bed, I lay down on it face up and reached behind me to grasp the headrail with both hands. I could still feel traces of Ashley's lubrication on the bar, and it excited me as I pulled my legs up and over my head, showing the crowd my bald pussy and ass. A few girls hollered their approval, and I spread my legs into a wide 'V' so they could see my glistening bald pussy more easily. A few people applauded my limber body, but after the previous week's sexy contortionist act, I knew they were looking for something more.

I caressed the insides of my thighs, stopping tantalizingly short of my pink folds, then turned around and placed my hips against the headboard, tilting my head as I peered at the audience upside down. They cheered loudly at my taunting gesture, knowing it was just a warm-up for the main act. Then I lifted my legs straight up above my body and slowly lowered them backwards toward my head. I'd been working on my flexibility in the weeks leading up to the performance and didn't have any difficulty resting my toes on the surface of the bed a few feet behind my head.

At this point all the audience could see was the slit of my ass with my face concealed by my closed legs. As they continued to cheer me on, I began to spread my feet apart until my legs were separated about sixty degrees. I could have easily spread them further apart, but that wasn't the main purpose of my routine. I placed the palms of my hands over each of my buttock cheeks and pulled my hips further down, moving my dripping pussy closer to my face.

With my toes inching further down toward the foot of the bed, the audience slowly began to realize what I was trying to do. As a loud murmur spread across the auditorium, I watched my slit move ever-closer to my puckering lips. With my erect clit quivering only inches from my mouth, I tilted my head back and peered toward the audience again, licking my lips in anticipation.

Realizing I was only inches away from taking my glistening gland into my mouth, their cheers grew in increasingly loud as I pressed my feet further down the mattress, lowering my box closer to my waiting mouth. Even though I'd practiced this hundreds of times before, knowing that so many eyes were watching me from the darkened auditorium raised my excitement to a whole new level. As my juices poured out of my slit over the top of my mound, I pulled my hips forward with one last tug, enveloping my hot gland with my moist lips.

A loud gasp suddenly arose from the audience, who'd never expected me to accomplish this feat of gymnastic elasticity. As I began to circle my tongue around my bright red jewel, a series of loud moans emanated from every corner of the auditorium. The crowd's reaction to my unique form of self-stimulation only increased my excitement as I lowered my hips even further, stroking my glistening slit up and down with my outstretched tongue. It was obvious that no one in the audience had ever seen anyone do anything remotely like this before, and I smiled as I listened to their shocked reaction.

As I licked the sides of my labia, pausing for long moments to suck my erect clit, I spread my legs further apart so they could see my pink pucker shining between my ass cheeks. I was putting every part of me out there for display, and the eroticism of the act lifted my passion with every passing moment. As I began to feel my pleasure rising toward its inevitable peak, I turned my face toward Ashley watching from the wings, and I nodded my head gently.

We'd both choreographed this routine carefully, and it was *her* I really wanted to cum with, not just the audience. Ashley dropped her robe on the floor and began walking onto the stage in my direction. When the audience saw that I'd enlisted an accomplice into my sexy act, their cheer rose even louder.

When Ashley reached the edge of my bed, she positioned herself behind my hips, peering down into my splayed, glistening slit. She smiled sexily at me, then grabbed one of her tits and leaned forward, stroking it against my wet opening. As she slid it toward my quivering mound, I popped my clit out of my mouth and began sucking on her nipple, alternating between her erect nub and mine. As the groans from the appreciative audience grew louder and louder, we smiled at each other, knowing we'd created something new and memorable.

But we were far from finished titillating the crowd, and I was still aching to come. I'd been holding back my orgasm until she joined me on the bed and as she peered into my glassy eyes, she pulled her body back until her face nestled directly between my thighs. While I resumed sucking my burning glans, she slowly licked my slit downward until she reached my pink rosebud. Without pausing for a second, she began circling my pucker with her long outstretched tongue, as my face began to turn redder and redder in mounting ecstasy.

As I felt my orgasm begin to wash over me, we locked eyes and I grunted loudly as my pussy began to clench in powerful contractions. I squirted my pent-up juices out of my pussy all over Ashley's pretty face embedded between my quivering cheeks. With my lips locked over my twitching clit and my entire body convulsing on the bed, I watched the muscles on the underside of my vulva pulsing as I sprayed squirt after squirt over Ashley's face mere inches in front of me.

The theater was now awash in the sounds of simultaneous orgasms as girls jilled themselves excitedly watching the two of us joined together in one of the sexiest routines they'd ever witnessed. Ashley reached between her legs and moaned into my crevasse as she popped off with the rest of the crowd. By the time I'd finished spraying her face and my clit stopped pulsing in my mouth, she leaned forward and kissed me passionately between my legs. As we lay there together for a long moment reveling in the reaction of the crowd, we nodded toward each other knowing we'd created a once-in-a-lifetime performance.

But we still had one ace up our sleeves to guarantee that at least one of us would be moving forward in the competition. With a sly grin, Ashley raised herself off the bed and straddled her feet between my hips as she peered down at my dripping crotch. Then she slowly squatted her body down until her ass cheeks rested against mine. I pulled my legs forward a few inches and bent my knees, tilting my hips backwards her until our pussies touched.

As we began to rock our bodies together, I watched her labia twisting and stretching against mine while we moaned in delirious pleasure. I was already buzzing from my last orgasm, and as we angled our hips toward one another, our clits touched and we gasped when we felt our sensitive organs melding together. As her slippery ass slid effortlessly over mine from our combined juices still coating our bodies, she reached down to hold my hands. I intertwined my fingers with hers as I peered into her eyes, feeling another powerful orgasm beginning to overtake me.

The feeling of her erect clit rolling over mine as our asses rubbed together was sublime. Although we'd experimented with the routine in the days leading up to this week's performance, there was something about the audacity of performing it live in front of a crowd of strangers that raised the excitement level even higher for both of us. As Ashley's mouth began to spread open while she approached another powerful orgasm, she peered down at me and mouthed the words *I love you*. By now, neither of us were paying any attention to the moans and groans emanating from the audience as we gripped each other's hands tightly while our pleasure consumed us.

Suddenly, Ashley let out a howl as her body began convulsing overtop of my hips. Watching her come with her pussy joined together with mine quickly put me over the edge also as I began spraying out in every direction from the tight seal between us. While I watched the spectacle from my prone position with my juices splashing all over our tits and faces, I saw my rosebud clamping rhythmically inches from my face. When we both finally finished shaking in a uniform mash of merged flesh, Ashley dropped down onto the bed beside me and kissed me gently.

"If *that* doesn't get us a free trip to the Desire resort in Mexico," she panted, "I don't know what will."

I peered over toward her and smiled.

"Who needs a trip to Mexico when we've got all the stimulation we need right here?"

VOLUME FOUR

THE DARE

1

———

"**D**o you have any more cases that need my help?" I asked my best friend and certified sex therapist, Hannah, at our weekly get-together lunch.

Ever since the last time she'd invited me to sit in on one of her sessions, I'd fantasized about watching another one of her clients release her inhibitions while learning how to orgasm for the first time.

"I'm afraid Haley was a one-off," Hannah said. "That was definitely pushing the envelope in terms of how far I can take the concept of a guided session."

"But you said many of your clients are open to the idea of using a surrogate to help them overcome their fear of intimacy?"

"Yes, but bringing a third party into the equation is stretching the limits of client confidentiality."

"Not if they agree to it up front and sign a consent form."

"True. But I'm already drifting into unchartered territory using this unconventional form of sex therapy. I'm supposed to just *talk* to them, not watch them while they touch themselves."

I shook my head as I sliced into my grilled salmon.

"You just want to have them all to *yourself*," I winked.

"Maybe," Hannah smiled, noisily sipping her margarita. "But my hands-on approach seems to be working."

"How's Haley doing these days, anyway?" I said, wondering about the pretty co-ed I'd shared an intimate encounter with. "Is she still receiving treatment?"

"The last I heard, she was in a committed relationship with another girl at college. She said her sex life was very satisfying. Apparently, that blended session with you helped her turn the corner."

"Glad I could help," I said, crossing my knees under the table to quiet my tingling clit as I remembered watching Haley come between my legs. "Happy to hear we cured another dysfunctional patient."

"You shouldn't be so dismissive of other women's problems," Hannah said, looking at me disapprovingly. "The inability to orgasm is far more prevalent than people think, especially among women. It's often caused by a traumatic episode in their past or severe childhood repression. Not everyone's as lucky as you and me to have had a healthy upbringing."

"I'm sorry," I said. "You're right. I remember how unsatisfying my first marriage was. We were both raised in a conservative household that frowned upon any form of sexual expression before marriage. All Jason seemed interested in was doing the missionary position in the dark. I hardly even had a chance to get aroused before he popped off. It wasn't until I discovered sex with other *women* that I really learned to enjoy myself."

"You're lucky that you found a successful outlet for your desires at a relatively young age," Hannah nodded. "You've come a long way since then."

"Literally and figuratively," I chuckled. "I can hardly believe how enjoyable my sex life has become. My orgasms are stronger and more powerful than I ever imagined. And the best part is how *long* I can make it last. It's almost like I can turn it on and off at will, holding out until the best optimal moment."

"You mean coming simultaneously with your partner?"

"Most of the time, yes. But sometimes I like to wait until *she's* finished coming so I can concentrate on maximizing her pleasure."

"Maybe you should become a partner in my therapy practice," Hannah said, lifting an eyebrow. "It sounds like you've mastered your art. I could use another colleague to juggle my growing caseload."

"Ha!" I chuckled. "I'm afraid I could never have your discipline. I'd want to jump the clients every time instead of just talking them through their process of self-discovery. You'd lose your license in no time if you brought me on as a full partner."

Hannah paused for a moment as she took another sip of her cocktail.

"Maybe we should *test* the premise and see just how disciplined you really are. You say you can turn your desire on and off at will. I bet you wouldn't be able to control yourself so easily under the right circumstances."

"How do you mean?" I said, suddenly intrigued. "Under what circumstances?"

Hannah peered at me with a devilish grin.

"I think if we put you in a highly charged sexual situation and took away your ability to control the level of stimulation you received, that I could make you pop off whenever I wanted."

"Like *what*?" I said, leaning forward on the table. "What did you have in mind?"

"I've actually been thinking about this for a while," Hannah smiled. "Ever since we were at this same restaurant and you tried out my new sex toy under the table. It gave me some fresh ideas for how we could take it to the next level."

"That was pretty fucking hot," I nodded, feeling my panties begin to dampen at the thought of Hannah watching me squirm in my seat while I was surrounded by restaurant patrons quietly eating their meals. "How could you possibly make that any more arousing?"

"You have *no* idea," Hannah smirked, lifting her glass back up to her lips.

2

———————

"You can't leave me hanging like that!" I huffed, slamming my fists down on the table. "What kind of evil plan are you cooking up?"

Hannah peered at me as she took another bite of her shrimp salad. She was enjoying torturing me while my mind raced trying to imagine what she was concocting. When she swallowed her mouthful and washed it down with another sip of wine, I looked at her pleadingly, holding up my hands up in despair.

"What if we made your next sexual encounter a *one-way* affair, instead of a partnered experience?" she said.

"I've already tried every type of self-stimulation, using every toy imaginable. I think I've mastered the art of orgasm control via masturbation many times."

"Not when somebody *else* is controlling the toy."

My eyes suddenly flew open as I began to realize what Hannah had in mind.

"You mean using some kind of remote-control device?" I said. "I've heard about those and always wanted to give it a try."

"But not in a public place," Hannah smiled.

"*What!*" I said, jerking back in my chair. "Why would you want to do that? Wouldn't you already have all the power you need controlling the level of stimulation I receive watching me one-on-one?"

"That would be too simple," she said. "Kind of like a staring contest. In the absence of any distractions, it would just be mind over matter. But in a public setting it won't be so easy for you to stay focused. Plus, the consequences will be more serious if you do lose control."

I leaned forward and calmly ate another bite of my salmon, pretending to be unfazed.

"In the unlikely event that you could actually force me to reach orgasm on your terms, I'd just bite my lip and cross my legs, and no one would be any the wiser."

Hannah speared another piece of shrimp and raised it to her mouth, sucking on it teasingly.

"You're forgetting about that *other* feature of your sexual powers, which is your tendency to squirt when you come. If I can make you come in a public place, it will be almost impossible for everyone to not know what's happening."

I placed my hands on the edge of the table and pushed my chair backwards, scrunching my face in dismay.

"You are truly evil," I said. "What kind of sick person would dream up such a crazy scenario?"

"Your best friend and lover, for one," Hannah smiled.

"*You're on!*" I said, slamming my cocktail down on the table. "But what's in it for me if I win? Do I get a silent stake in your practice?"

"I think it's best we continue your role as a special consultant. I think we can use you more effectively as a mutual participant when the need arises. I was thinking of something we can *both* enjoy."

"Such as?"

"We've both talked about you much we'd love to go to Bora Bora. If I can make you lose control in public, you'll have to pay for the airfare. But if you're as good as you say you are, then *I'll* pay for the flights. What do you say–are you up for the challenge?"

"Possibly," I said, getting wetter by the moment imagining Hannah's crazy idea. "But exactly what kind of public settings are we talking about? It's only fair that you let me know what I'm getting myself into before I take the leap."

"No dice," Hannah said, crossing her arms. "If you're as skilled as you're making yourself out to be, it shouldn't matter what the setting is. Half the fun will be in your not knowing until we get there."

I paused for a long moment, running my eyes over Hannah's face, trying to divine her thoughts.

"Fine," I said, holding out my hand across the table. "But this'll be quite a switch for you–encouraging a client *not* to reach orgasm for a change."

"Quite the contrary," Hannah smiled, clasping my hand. "It's fully aligned with the vision of my practice. I've never yet had a client who failed to achieve sexual fulfillment. But as I always like to tell them—most of the fun is in the process of *getting* there."

3

"Okay, so now that I'm committed, tell me where you had in mind for this little experiment."

"Actually," Hannah said, "I have a *series* of places in mind, each one more challenging than the one before."

"But I thought you said this was a one-off proposition?"

"I said nothing of the sort. I only said that if you won, I'd pay for the flights to Bora Bora. If you want me to cover the cost of hotels, food, and all the other incidentals, you'll have to pass progressively tougher tests. We don't want to make this *too* easy for you, do we?"

I crossed my arms and huffed, putting on my best pouty face.

"It hardly seems fair," I said. "But I'm still game. Besides, either one of us can pull out at any time to lock in our gains, right?"

"I suppose so," Hannah shrugged. "But what would be the fun in that? Something tells me once you've tried the first experiment, you won't want to stop. I think you're going to find this whole thing quite titillating and exciting. This will be the most fun either one of us has had in a long time."

I pushed the rest of my half-eaten salmon dish to the side, suddenly no longer interested in eating.

"Okay, lay it on me then. Where are you planning to take me for the first test?

Hannah gulped down the rest of her margarita then peered at me with a lopsided grin.

"Church. More specifically, a *Catholic* church. You haven't been in quite a while, have you? This will be your chance to repent and atone for all your sins."

"It's not like I've broken any commandments or anything–"

"The Catholic Church still considers sex outside of marriage a mortal sin. So technically, you've been doing a ton of sinning since your marriage ended."

"Well I haven't been a practicing Catholic for ages," I snorted. "So my conscience is clear. This'll be a cakewalk. All I have to do is sit quietly in my pew, right?"

"Yes, but it'll be a *front-row* pew, in full view of the priest who'll be delivering the sermon."

"Okay, but I'll be fully clothed, right? It's not like there'll be anything for him to see..."

"Not if you can keep your composure and don't cum all over the floor," Hannah said, cocking her head playfully.

"I don't think I'll have any difficulty keeping my dick in my pants, in a manner of speaking. But you raise a good point. You can't expect me not to get a little wet while you're stimulating me. What will I be allowed to wear?"

"I assume you'll dress appropriately, wearing your Sunday best. A mid-length skirt and button-up blouse should do the trick. You should be able to hide a few dribbles that way, right?"

"I suppose so, but how will we muffle the sound of the vibrator buzzing inside my panties? There's likely to be other people sitting around me in adjacent pews..."

"Never fear," Hannah smiled, reaching into her purse and pulling out a U-shaped silicone sex toy. "I've been talking with our friend at the local Babeland store. She's given me the latest prototype of the We-Vibe vibrator to test." She held up a smaller device with two control buttons and a flywheel. "Complete with a Bluetooth remote control. And the best thing is that it's whisper-quiet.

"Here," she said, handing me the flexible device. "See for yourself."

She tapped one of the buttons on the remote and the thick side of the contraption began buzzing softly in my hand.

"Okay," I nodded, looking around me to see if any other restaurant patrons were distracted by the gentle hum of the object. "It's *quiet* enough, but which end goes inside?"

"The bulbous end is a natural G-spot stimulator. You place the flatter end against your clit, then pull the thing up tight against your vulva to keep it snugly in place."

I suddenly became mindful of the wetness permeating my panties as I imagined the device vibrating inside me, surrounded by a bunch of oblivious bystanders.

"Can I give it a try here, like we did last time?" I grinned.

"No way," Hannah said, pulling the toy out of my hands. "There'll be no trial runs for this or any future tests. You'll just have to wait until we get to the church."

"And where will *you* be sitting while this is all going down?" I said.

"Right next to you, of course. I'll want a front-row seat to watch all the action."

On Sunday morning, Hannah picked me up and drove me the two miles to our local church. The entire time I squirmed in my seat trying to imagine what it would be like having a vibrator buzzing inside me in the quiet chapel. When we got to the church parking lot, she pulled into a sheltered space then plucked the blue vibrator out of her purse and handed it to me, resting her arm on the seat cushion expectantly.

"*What?*" I said. "You don't trust me to put it in privately?"

"Not really," she smirked. "For all I know, you might pull on some adult diapers under your skirt to hide any unintended releases. Here," she said, handing me a plastic vial. "I brought some lube to make it go in easier."

"I don't need any," I said, pulling the vibrator out of her hands and placing it under my skirt. "I'm already plenty worked up thinking about this scenario."

"I hope you're wearing panties under that skirt," Hannah said, watching me shift my weight as I placed the device against my vulva. "We wouldn't want it popping out at an inopportune moment."

"I'll just have to leave that up to your imagination," I sneered, lifting my skirt halfway up my thigh. "Unless you need to inspect the goods to make sure I'm not cheating."

"I trust you," Hannah smiled, opening her car door. "Something tells me you're looking forward to this just as much as I am."

As we approached the entrance to the church, I noticed a familiar figure standing at the top of the steps greeting the incoming parishioners, and he made eye contact with me when Hannah and I approached the landing.

"Jade!" Father Fife said, holding out his hands to me. "I haven't seen you in such a long time. It's so good to have you join us again."

"I'm sorry, Father," I said, placing my sweaty hand between his. "I've been a little distracted lately..."

"Life has a habit of getting in the way of the important things," he said. "We're just glad to have you whenever you can find time." He turned to Hannah, raising his eyebrows in curiosity. "And who's this lovely lady you've brought with you to attend our service today?"

"This is Hannah," I said, motioning toward my friend. "I thought I'd bring her along for moral support."

"Happy to have you, Hannah," Father Fife said, clasping Hannah's hands warmly. "The Lord knows we all need moral support wherever we can find it."

Hannah nodded politely, then the two of us walked through the entrance doors where I dipped my hand into the bowl of holy water and crossed my chest before continuing on toward the front of the chapel.

"*Jesus*," Hannah whispered, peering around the imposing shrine.

"Is it just me, or did that feel a little creepy? All that talk about *having* us and that prolonged hand-holding. Hasn't he been paying any attention to the me-too movement?"

"I'm not sure any of that applies to men of the *cloth*," I chuckled. "But you better be careful about using the Lord's name like that around here. If anybody overhears you, you're liable to be burned at the stake."

The two of us stepped lively down the main aisle and finding a free spot in the front row, we took our seats flanked by two elderly couples. It was hard to imagine how Hannah would be able to use the remote-control device sandwiched so closely between other parishioners, and I crossed my legs, thankful for the brief respite. When everyone had filed into the chapel and the bell signaled the start of the service, a hush fell over the chamber and we all stood up as Father Fife walked onto the pulpit in his flowing robes.

"In the name of the Father, and of the Son, and of the Holy Spirit," he intoned solemnly.

"Amen," the congregation murmured in unison.

"The Lord be with you," he said.

"And with your spirit," the couples beside me retorted.

What the hell have I gotten myself into? I thought, feeling the flexible vibrator pressing against the inside of my closed legs. I didn't consider myself a terribly religious person, but being in this holy place surrounded by all the familiar rituals brought back all the old memories from my parents about the consequences of sinful behavior. *Surely getting secretly stimulated by a sex toy in the house of God will send me straight to hell.*

This was the point in the church service where everybody was supposed to take a moment to make a penitential act. While I listened to the other parishioners around me making their supplications, my knees began shaking as I made my own silent prayer for forgiveness.

"May Almighty God have mercy on us all," the priest said. "Forgive us our sins, and bring us to everlasting life."

"Amen," I joined in the congregation's response.

"Let us pray," Father Fife said, bowing his head.

As we closed our eyes and he began his opening prayer, Hannah nudged me with her knee and my mind raced with images of the pastor scornfully looking down at us while we played our blasphemous game. I peered up as he flapped his Bible closed, and caught him glancing in my direction.

"Through our Lord Jesus Christ, your Son," he said. "Who lives and reigns with you in the unity of the Holy Spirit, one God forever and ever."

"Amen," I said aloud, hoping he'd see me behaving like a good Catholic girl and turn his attention elsewhere.

He motioned for everyone to sit down and I was glad to get off my shaky feet onto the relative safety of the wooden pew.

"Good morning, ladies and gentlemen," he began his homily. "Today, I would like to talk with you about *morality*. Specifically, about the decaying state of society's morals in today's world. All around us we are surrounded by prurient symbols of modern decadence. First it was in the form of the printed word, then motion pictures, then the ubiquitous internet. It seems everywhere we turn, we are bombarded with profane and sacrilegious images."

I felt my heart pounding in my chest, like he was singling me out personally for my not-so-infrequent porn surfing.

"We seem to have forgotten," he railed, "the Lord's commandment that we shall not covet thy neighbor's wife. This admonition can be taken in its broadest context. Not only have many of you forsaken the sacred institution of marriage, but the egregious and widespread popularity of obscene *pornography* belies our unbridled lust and depravity. God slew Onan for spilling his seed, and so He will strike all others who practice self-abuse."

Hannah nudged her knee against mine, suddenly reminding me why we were here. I was glad that she hadn't yet had the opportunity to take out her remote-control device, and I prayed that we'd be able to get through most of the service without her rudely interrupting it. I'd already begun to regret agreeing to this little venture, and I hoped that somehow we'd be able to bypass this first phase in her experiment.

"I'd like you to pick up your Bibles," Father Fife said, interrupting my thoughts. "And turn to Mark, Chapter 7, Verse 20."

Hannah and I reached down to pick up the bibles lying on the seat beside each of us, and we flipped to the indicated section.

"Read this passage with me, my friends," Father Fife instructed. "What comes *out* of a person is what defiles him," he enunciated, while the congregation quietly murmured along.

As I began to recite the passage along with him, I saw Hannah reach into her side pocket and place her closed hand between the book binding.

"For from within come evil thoughts," I continued reading as I peered out of the corner of my eye to see what she was up to.

"Sexual immorality, adultery, coveting, wickedness..." we read in unison.

Suddenly, I felt the interior end of the vibrator begin to tremble inside me and I stuttered, trying to finish the passage.

"Deceit...sensuality...envy..." I stammered, trying to catch my breath as I followed along. Hearing my labored recital, Hannah turned her head in my direction, acknowledging my silent suffering. She knew exactly what I was feeling and how difficult it was for me to remain composed as I read the script.

"All these evil things...come from *within*," I gulped as I began to feel the pleasure spread across my pelvic region. "And they defile a person."

"Consider these words carefully," the priest said, surveying my hunched-over posture. "For the Lord does not abide salacious thoughts and behavior. If you want passage into His Kingdom, you must be as pure and righteous as He."

He paused for a moment to let the message sink in, then he motioned with his two hands for us to be seated. I was grateful for the rest, and I froze upright in my chair trying to ignore the movement of the possessed instrument inside me.

"Let us consider for a moment *another* one of God's ten commandments," Father Fife continued. "Thou shall not commit *adultery*. The Lord made Eve from the flesh of Adam, and in so doing signified that forever more man shall be united to his wife as one..."

As Father Fife ramped up the intensity of his gayphobic critique, so did Hannah, furtively adjusting the flywheel on the remote-control device nestled under her palm in her lap. As she slowly increased the speed of the vibrations emanating inside my pussy, I squirmed on the bench, trying to restrain my rising passion.

"By rejecting the sanctity of marriage," Father Fife continued, glancing distractedly in my direction, "you have all *sinned*. In the book of Deuteronomy, we saw that God ordered adulterers be stoned to death. For your indiscriminate behavior, so shall the Lord indiscriminately smite thee."

Jesus, I thought. If that's what awaits a sinner for cheating on their spouse, I wonder what happens to someone who self-abuses herself while sitting for Sunday Service in a house of God. *Surely I'll burn in hell for this act of sacrilege.*

Just when I thought I was beginning to get control over the delicious sensations stimulating my insides, Father Fife instructed us to stand once again and recite another passage from the Bible.

"Please stand now and read Peter 1:16 with me," he said.

Everyone stood and dutifully flipped to the relevant section of the scriptures. This time it was even harder for me to stand motionless, as my knees fluttered unsteadily from the pleasurable sensations radiating inside me.

"It is written..." I tried to read along. "That you shall be holy, for I am holy."

I saw Hannah's hands moving once again inside her prayer book, and suddenly I felt the *other* end of the U-shaped vibrator buzzing against my clit.

"And now Galatians 5:16," Father Fife instructed, barely giving me a chance to recover.

I flipped to the new citation and gasped for breath as my legs wobbled beneath me.

"But I say," I panted unsteadily. "Walk by the Spirit, and you will not gratify the desires of the flesh."

"So it is written," Father Fife said, closing his Bible. "Be righteous as the Lord, and you shall join him in Heaven for everlasting days. And now," he said, magnifying my torture. "I would like us to sing together one of my favorite hymns celebrating His blessing, *Amazing Grace*. Please pick up your hymn books and turn to page forty-three."

"Amazing grace, how sweet the sound," the priest began to sing as the entire congregation joined him in harmony.

"That saved a wretch like me," I sang along, trying to ignore the message that seemed targeted directly at me. As I tried to hold the melody, Hannah cupped the remote-control device in her hand and turned the flywheel to its maximum setting.

"I once was lost, but now am found," I hyperventilated, pressing my legs together as hard as I could to stifle the rising passion that threatened to overtake me.

"Was blind, but now I see," I squealed, singing the last word decidedly off-pitch as Father Fife turned to see my entire body shaking as I belted the famous hymn.

By the time I'd finished the song, I'd somehow managed to keep it together and fight off the cresting passion that had threatened to put me over the edge. When we finally sat back down, Hannah mercifully turned the vibrator off, and I spread my hands over my ruffled skirt to signal that I'd managed to keep myself composed.

When the service was over and we walked up the aisle behind the rest of the assembly to exit the church, I couldn't wait to get out of the building to wash myself off, figuratively and literally. I was glad that we were at the back of the crowd so nobody could see the back of my skirt. I wasn't sure if my leaking pussy had left a stain, but I sure as hell didn't want one of the parishioners pointing it out. When we finally exited the entrance doors, Father Fife turned to the two of us and smiled.

"I noticed you seemed a little more passionate than usual reciting today's passages, Jade" he said to me.

"Yes, Father," I said, shaking his hand unsteadily. "I felt truly embodied by the spirit."

"And *you*, Hannah," he nodded. "Did you enjoy today's service also?"

"Oh yes," she said. "It was the most moving sermon I've attended in a long time."

"I hope you'll both come again," Father Fife said to the two of us.

"I'm sure we *will*, Father," Hannah smiled as we continued down the steps.

Like the second we get back home, I thought to myself, dying to tear off my clothes and squirt all over Hannah's face while she ate out my still-dripping pussy.

4

———

"So what did you think?" Hannah said once we got in the car. "Did you find the experience uplifting?"

"I think you're *evil*," I said, reaching under my dress and pulling the vibrator out of my pussy. "You know we're both going to *hell* for that."

"At least we'll know how to enjoy ourselves once we get there," Hannah smirked.

"So, did I pass the test?" I said, inspecting the toy that had caused me so much torture minutes earlier.

"That was pretty impressive," Hannah nodded. "I particularly enjoyed watching you try to finish singing Amazing Grace."

"I practically burst a gasket during that one. Especially when Father Fife looked in my direction."

"That was fucking hilarious," Hannah laughed. "I loved his comment about how *moved* you seemed by the service. I still can't believe he didn't suspect any foul play."

"Maybe he *did*, but he was too embarrassed to admit it. Either way, I'll never be able to show my face again in this church after that little stunt. If *he* doesn't strike me down, then surely the Lord on high will."

"But it was worth it though, right?" Hannah said, angling out of the church parking lot. "It was insanely hot watching you shudder and squirm during the prayers and recitals. Didn't you find it incredibly exciting trying to control yourself in public?"

"How can you be so sure I *did*?" I said, flexing the U-shaped vibrator in my hands. "Maybe I experienced my own little rapture when you weren't looking."

"Oh *please*," Hannah said, stopping at the turnoff to my subdivision. "You don't think I *know* you by now after all the times we've made love? You were never good at hiding your orgasms. Besides your noisy vocalizations, you have a distinct way of contorting your body when you come. Not to mention the tidal wave you produce after a long buildup. Father Fife would have had to send in *Noah's Ark* to save all the believers once you opened the floodgates."

"Speaking of..." I said, placing my hand between her legs as she pulled into my driveway. "If you don't finish what you started, I'm going to spring a leak. Now be a good girl while I sit on your face."

Hannah and I rushed upstairs, where it only took a few seconds for me to pop off while she sucked my aching clit into her mouth. After we both came hard reliving the excitement of the church experience, we flopped back down onto the bed, giggling like two little girls.

"Thanks," I panted. "I needed that."

"That was pretty crazy, wasn't it?" she said. "I still can't believe we got away with it. Front row seat and all."

I rolled over onto my side and propped my head on my elbow as I peered into her eyes.

"It's pretty hard to imagine how you'll be able to step it up after that. What could possibly be harder than trying to hide having sex in a church?"

"Actually, if you think about it, that was almost too easy. After all, hardly anybody was looking at you the whole time. Everybody was focused on the priest or their prayer books. All you had to do was bite your lip and squeeze your legs together under your dress. At the *next* venue, people are going to have a harder time keeping their eyes off of you."

"Why?" I said, darting my eyes over her face trying to imagine what she was scheming. "Are you going to have me sing karaoke or put me in a wet t-shirt contest or something?"

"Not quite," she smiled. "But those aren't bad ideas. No, this next time you're going to be in a public library."

"That doesn't sound so difficult," I said, pulling back. "Everybody will be busy reading a book or searching the stacks."

"Oh, they'll be searching the *stacks* alright," she said, peering down at my plump breasts. "The way I'm going to have you dressed, not many people will be focused on *reading*. Plus, this time there won't be the sound of the preacher's voice or the congregation's singing to cover up your moans and groans. It'll be quiet as a mouse in there."

"Okay..." I said, trying to imagine myself in this new setting. "But where will you be this time?"

"I'll be at an adjacent table, providing a whole *different* kind of kind of distraction."

"No problem," I huffed. "I'll just close my eyes and think about dead cats or something."

"Uh-uh," Hannah said, shaking her head and blinking her eyes at me playfully. "You've got to be fully present in the moment if you want to prove you can control yourself. The whole point of these public displays is for you to show that you can turn it on and off as easily as you said you could."

"Fine," I said. "But you keep adding all these restrictions. What *other* ground rules do I need to know about?"

"You just need to look at me for the duration of the test. *All* of me— both what's going on above and below the table. And you have to remain upright in your seat the whole time. No slouching and trying to hide your best assets."

"You're such a *tease!*" I said, leaning in to bite her nipples. "How long do I have to do this? You can't possibly torture me any longer than the hour you just put me through at the church service."

Hannah cradled my head and wiggled her body down until we made eye contact again.

"Since we'll be ramping up the *other* sources of distraction, I suppose it's only fair that we cut down on the length of this test. Do you think you can survive a half hour without coming?"

"*Pshaw!*" I snorted. "After the church experience, this'll be a cakewalk. When were you thinking of doing this?"

Hannah paused for a moment to consider her options.

"The libraries are busiest on the weekends, but we don't want too many distractions stealing attention away from your performance. How about Wednesday afternoon around three in the afternoon? There should be just enough mid-day traffic around that time to keep everybody amused."

"You're on!" I said, rolling on top of her, pressing my mound against her pussy. "But you don't mind if I try to build up my immunity before then, do you? I figure the more cums I can get in ahead of time, the easier it will be to stem the floodwaters."

"By all means," she said, spreading her legs and tilting her hips until our clits touched. "I want to enjoy living out the fantasy as much as *you* do."

On the day of the library visit, Hannah came over to my place an hour early to supervise my preparation. She wanted to make sure I was dressed provocatively enough to attract the attention of the library visitors, both male and female. After trying on a variety of outfits, she finally settled on a tight-fitting tube-top and miniskirt with no underwear. Although my naughty parts were covered up by the opaque fabric, my ample-sized tits and curvy hips left little to the imagination as to what was underneath. This time, I'd be letting it all hang out for everyone to see.

When we got to the library, Hannah found an open table for me to sit in the main atrium, then she positioned herself at an adjacent table about ten feet away. I found a thick textbook resting on the counter and I pulled it over in front of me, hoping to block the view of my pointy tits protruding out of my stretchy tube top. At first, the library was thinly populated, and I shook my head impatiently, wondering what was keeping her from getting started. I was eager to complete the test before it got too busy, but she simply smiled back at me, spreading her legs slowly to reveal her bald pussy. She'd obviously scoped out the place ahead of time, and I scowled at her for making my task even more difficult.

Within ten minutes or so, the library began to fill up as students and office workers began to flit in after class and work hours. A pretty co-ed took a seat kitty-corner to me at my table, while a young stud in an expensive suit plopped some law books down on the table next to Hannah. Whether he was more interested in securing a position to see *me* better or to be next to Hannah, was unclear. Either way, both of them would have prime viewing access to me from their positions.

After tapping out a few messages on their phones, the two visitors opened their books and lowered their heads to begin reading. Within seconds, I felt the familiar tremble of the vibrator fluttering inside me, and I jumped in surprise. The pretty co-ed peered up at me with pinched eyebrows and I turned the page in my encyclopedia, pretending to be absorbed in my reading material. Suddenly, I felt the buzzing sensation of the *internal* branch of the vibrator turn to maximum and I jerked my head up to stare at Hannah in protest. She shook her head disapprovingly, while motioning with her two fingers to keep my gaze focused on her.

I nodded in capitulation, and she dimmed the vibration setting back to low. The well-dressed lawyer occasionally glanced up at me, darting his eyes back and forth between my tight bosom and my bare knees under the table. Hannah smiled when she recognized his attention as she toggled the remote control vibration settings in the palm of her hand.

While the pleasurable sensations began to spread over my pelvic region, I struggled to keep myself still in my seat watching Hannah's slit widening as she spread her legs further apart. When she suddenly turned on the clitoral vibration setting, I emitted a little squeak, and the young blonde girl looked up at me, pursing her lips to say "*Shhh!*"

"Sorry," I whispered, rubbing my hand over my exposed belly. "I've got a bit of an upset stomach."

She shook her head and returned to reading her book. But the direct stimulation on my clit had dramatically increased my pleasure and my knees began to part unconsciously. The handsome hunk looked up from his law books when he noticed the movement and peered under the table as I struggled to keep my knees from fluttering in excitement.

Hannah noticed the dynamic going on between the two of us, and when the hunk temporarily looked back down, she reached into the pocket of her dress and pulled out a long rubber dildo. As I watched her with glassy eyes, she slowly inserted the dong into her snatch and began to stroke it in and out of her hole. I shook my head at her to show my anger at her tormenting me, but she smiled back at me, sensuously licking her lips. She knew how much I liked to trib using a double-sided dildo, and as she rocked her hips slowly under the table, she took her hand off the shaft while the other end wobbled tantalizing in my direction.

I mouthed the words *Fuck You*, and she responded by saying *Yes Please*. As much as I tried to resist it, as she began to increase the speed of the clitoral massager, my legs continued to spread apart with a mind of their own. Before long, the handsome lawyer looked up at me again, this time his gaze squarely focused between my legs.

I knew he could probably see me just as well as I could see Hannah an equal distance away, and his eyes widened when he saw the strange blue device planted between my legs. Suddenly, he brought his hand under the table to adjust himself, and I noticed his pole tenting in his pants. As his lengthening hard-on snaked up the front of his hips, I dribbled down the side of my legs, admiring his impressive package. I grunted unconsciously watching his visceral reaction, and the pretty co-ed sitting next to me looked up again, shaking her head.

"Why don't you go to the *washroom* if you're not feeling well?" she said. "This is a library!"

"I'm sorry," I said, clutching my stomach. "I think it's something I ate. I'll be finished my research soon, then I'll leave."

The girl looked at my trembling tummy suspiciously, then returned to reading her book. When I peered over again at the hunky lawyer, I saw that he'd unzipped his pants, with his large dick poking straight up toward the underside of his table. Nobody else could have seen what he was doing from my vantage point, and he smiled at me as I spread my legs wider apart in sympathy. Part of me wanted to close my knees and hide the vibrator rumbling inside me, but when I saw him reach under the table and begin to stroke his cock, I couldn't help groaning as I imagined myself planted on top of him.

The girl looked up again, but seeing the strange look on my face as I peered at the hunk across the aisle, she traced my gaze over to him and gasped when she saw what he was doing under the table. After pausing for a moment, she looked back at me and smiled as she lowered her arm under the table and began to move her hand between her legs. I glanced over at Hannah and saw the big rubber dildo glistening from her juices while she watched the three-way action that was happening between our two tables.

As much as I tried to ignore the rising passion emanating from my twitching pussy, it was impossible to avoid the sight of the three beauties stimulating themselves while they watched me squirm and moan with the U-shaped vibrator stimulating every part of my dripping crotch. As the handsome hunk began jerking himself more forcefully under the table, my gaze shifted back to the pretty co-ed, whose cheeks were beginning to flush from the pleasure she was experiencing under the table. With the four of us nearing a mutual crescendo, I suddenly flashed back to my childhood, when my grandmother used to read bedtime stories to me.

Goodnight moon, I said to myself, trying to remember the words to my favorite story in an effort to shift my focus away from erotic scene unfolding before me. *Good night, cow jumping over the moon.*

When I refocused my gaze, I saw Hannah slumping in her chair with her legs spread wide apart, reaming herself with two hands tightly gripped around the shaft of the glistening dildo.

Good night kittens, good night mittens, I said to myself, trying to think of anything other than the sight of these three hotties rimming themselves in the middle of the public library. Whether each of them was fully aware of what the other was doing, from my perspective the sight of them pleasuring themselves together was impossible to resist.

I glanced at the pretty co-ed, and she looked me straight in the eye as a bright flush spread over her cheeks. When I turned back toward the hunky lawyer, he suddenly stopped moving his hand as he gripped his purple crown in his fist, spewing long ropes of cum all over the underside of the table.

Good night, bear. Good night, chairs, I murmured quickly under my breath.

When the girl saw the guy spurting cum out of his huge dick, she hunched over and gasped, jerking rhythmically in her seat. Seeing the other two coming so hard only a few feet away from me, Hannah groaned softly as she pulled the rubber dildo deep into her pussy, flapping her knees uncontrollably.

Good night, stars. Good night, air. Good night, noises everywhere, I said, feeling my juices streaming steadily down the insides of my legs.

5

———

"*N*o *fair!*" I protested when Hannah and I left the library. "You get to have all the fun while I suffer in silence!"

"I never said *I* couldn't come while you were doing these tests," Hannah smiled. "That's half the attraction. Nothing turns me on more than watching you twist and squirm while I stimulate you from a distance."

"*Give* me that fucking thing," I said, tearing the remote control device from her hand. "I don't want to wait another second to get off."

"Right *here*?" Hannah said, looking around the library entrance at the passing patrons.

"Why not? I've already had sex in two public places. What difference will it make if I do it *outside*?"

I peered around me and saw a small alcove near an emergency exit behind a stand of bushes.

"There's a relatively secluded spot over there. You can be my lookout."

"Fuck that," Hannah said, grabbing my hand, pulling me behind the hedge. "I want a piece of this too."

We ducked into the doorway, pressing our bodies together and I flicked on the remote control switch. Hannah reached down and pulled the vibrator out of my pussy, then reinserted each end into our separate holes.

"There's more than *one* way to use this flexible toy," she smiled.

"Except *this* time," I said, "I'll be in charge of controlling the level of stimulation."

I tapped the two buttons on the controller then adjusted the flywheels to their maximum setting. Hannah lifted the front of our skirts and pressed her mound against mine, kissing me passionately. Even though I only had half of the U-shaped vibrator throbbing against me, the action of Hannah's mound grinding up against my own provided more than enough clitoral stimulation. As we thrust our tongues into each other's mouths, I reached under Hannah's dress and grabbed her buttocks, pulling her hard against me.

"I'm going to cum all over your little twat," I said, feeling my orgasm rising within me like a powerful volcano.

"Let it go, girl," Hannah said.

I lifted my knee and wrapped my leg around her ass, pointing my vulva against her mound.

"Uhnn," I groaned. "Here it comes. *Fuckkkk!*"

As my pussy clamped down over the fat end of the vibrator, I squirted my pent-up juices out the sides of my slit all over Hannah's abdomen as we shook in each other's arms from the combined stimulation of the curved wand.

"*Fuck me*," Hannah said as we collapsed against the side of the door with our juices streaming down the insides of our legs. "I never even thought about using this as a double-sided dildo."

"How do *you* like not being in control for a change?" I said, raising my eyebrows in protest. "Now you know what I've been going through these last two episodes."

"I have a whole new respect for what you've been able to accomplish," she nodded. "Especially with those two hotties jerking off right next to you."

"You have no idea," I said. "That hunk sitting next to you was hung like a horse. You should have seen him when he finally dumped his load. I thought he'd never stop coming underneath the desk."

"I guess the clean-up crew will have more than a few wads of gum to scrape of the bottom of the table next time," Hannah chuckled. "But I was more focused on the cute girl sitting beside you. She certainly changed her tune when she finally figured out what was going on."

"When I saw the sex flush roll over her cheeks, it took every ounce of my willpower not to come along with her."

"How *did* you manage to keep it together?" Hannah asked. "I thought you were really going to lose control this time."

"I just transported myself somewhere else and tried to think of something as far removed from my predicament as possible."

"Well, whatever it was, it seemed to work. Though I dare say the three of *us* more than made up for your lack of enthusiasm. I haven't come that hard in ages."

"So what now?" I said. "Now that I've managed to get the hotel and airfare paid for, what do I have to do to cover the meals for our trip to Bora Bora?"

Hannah pulled the vibrator out of our pussies and leaned against the opposite wall of the alcove as she looked at me with a sly smile.

"We have to step it *up* another notch, right? Both of these times you were fully clothed and had a few props to distract attention from what was going on down there. This next time, you're going to be completely *naked*."

I shook my head and peered at her with a quizzical look.

"Are you taking me to a nude beach or something?"

"Even better," she smirked. "You're going to be a nude model for a college art class."

"What the–" I gasped, feeling my pussy twitch one last time, sending another stream of juices running down my leg.

For the next week or so, all I could think about was what it would be like to stand in front of a group of strangers while they sketched me in the nude. As much as I tried to get more details from

Hannah, she refused to give me any more information until we arrived at the studio. I wasn't exactly sure how she was going to pull off stimulating me from a distance with a vibrator sticking out of my pussy. But every time I thought about it, I stood in front of my full-length dressing mirror imagining everyone watching me while I jilled myself to orgasm.

On the scheduled appointment day, Hannah drove me to the local college, where we met with the art professor to go over the ground rules for the session. The prof was younger and prettier than I imagined, and I sat in rapt attention while she explained how it all worked.

"Hi, I'm Danielle," she said, introducing herself to the two of us.

"Jade," I said, extending my hand.

"Hannah," my partner-in-crime said.

"Which one of you will be posing today?"

I held up my hand meekly.

"I'm just here for moral support," Hannah smiled.

"The protocol is pretty straight-forward," Danielle said. "We'll keep you covered up until everyone is ready to begin. Then I'll ask you to hold a pose for about thirty minutes while the students draw you in the nude. I'll be circulating around the room during this time, offering feedback and critique on their compositions. The most important thing is for you to try to remain as still as possible for the duration of the assignment."

While she was talking to the two of us, I stole occasional glances at her figure. She was wearing a tight-fitting mid-length skirt and a white cotton blouse partially unbuttoned at the neck. Her breasts were full and round, and my gaze kept falling to her sexy cleavage and her toned legs crossed at the knee. By the time she finished her briefing, I could feel the heat emanating from my throbbing pussy.

"Did you have any questions?" she asked.

"How many people are we expecting to show up?" I asked nervously.

"We have twenty students in my class, and I expect most of them to show up for this assignment. This is one of the more popular electives."

"I can see why," Hannah said, eyeing my curvy figure under my robe.

"And I can't cover up any part of my body?" I said.

"That's the whole point of figure drawing," Danielle said. "To sketch the subject in his or her full glory."

"Don't people sometimes get–um–*excited* with so many eyes on their naked body?" I said, wondering especially how a male model would manage to keep himself composed in this situation.

"I tell both the models and the artists that it's perfectly normal and natural. That's part of the challenge–to capture their feelings and emotions in a still composition."

"May I participate in the session also?" Hannah asked. "I mean as an *artist*. I've always wanted to sketch Jade in the nude."

"Of course," Danielle said. "I only ask that you try not to distract the model with any overt comments or expressions."

"I wouldn't *dream* of it," Hannah smiled.

"Okay," the professor said. "Why don't you take a few minutes to freshen up and prepare yourself while the students get set up?"

Hannah and I walked out into the hallway where we found a private washroom, locking the door behind us.

"Okay," I said, crossing my arms impatiently. "How exactly are you going to pull this off with everyone staring at my naked pussy?"

"Never fear, my pretty," Hannah cooed, taking a small dumbbell-shaped object out of her purse. "These are a special type of Ben-wa balls. They vibrate in different ways, depending on how I adjust the controller. Everything's going to be hiding *inside* you this time. No one will be any the wiser as to what's going on, unless you give them reason to suspect otherwise."

"Ben-wa balls," I nodded, reflecting back on the time I'd used them in the airplane lavatory with my Swedish stewardess friends. "Ingenious."

"You shouldn't have any trouble controlling yourself with *these* things, right?" Hannah said, raising a playful eyebrow. "Only one *part* of you is going to be stimulated this time."

"Well, as you've explained to me many times, the main body of my clitoris is actually located on the *inside* of my vagina, not the outside. And I've already had some experience with these things. So *no*, it's not going to be any easier to control myself."

"Well this should be all the more interesting then," Hannah smiled, reaching under my robe and inserting the chrome balls into my slit.

When we returned to the studio, the classroom had already filled up with students, and the instructor motioned for everyone to take their seats. There was an even mix of men and women, and they were all young and cute. As Danielle introduced me to the class, I scanned around the room, feeling my pussy throb as I made eye contact with each student.

In the front row, a pretty brunette with a cute ponytail smiled at me as I glanced at her tawny thighs exposed in cut-off jeans under her tilted drafting table. Directly behind her, a cute redhead with little freckles sprinkled over her nose peered up at me, gazing at my excited nipples poking two darts in the soft fabric of my robe. As I traced a line further toward the back of the room, I saw an African-American man looking like a young Denzel Washington nodding at me as he admired my curvy figure.

Fuck me, I thought. *They're not going to make this any easier for me.*

As I imagined fucking each one of them in turn, the professor interrupted my thoughts with final instructions to the group.

"Because of the personal nature of this session, I'll ask everyone to place their phones in their pockets or purses to protect the privacy of our subject. You all know the protocol for drawing the model, which I've already explained to Jade, so if you'd like to take out your drawing materials now, we can begin. Jade, if you feel comfortable, you may disrobe now and sit comfortably on the stool."

The professor motioned to an adjacent chair, and I pulled off my robe and sat awkwardly on the bench with my feet propped up on the lower bar and my knees clamped tightly together.

"You may wish to turn your body a few degrees to your left," Danielle instructed, "so our students can depict a partial side profile. Try to relax your legs by placing one foot on the floor and the other on the lower foot rest. As far as your hands, most models find it most comfortable to rest them in their lap. Since we'll need you to remain as still as possible for the duration of the session, you may find it useful to find a focal point somewhere in the room where you can fix your gaze. Are we ready to begin?"

I nodded my head and scanned the back wall, seeing a message board above the African-American student's head. A sign listed the ten meeting norms to optimize productivity, and I began to read them quietly to myself to distract attention from the twenty sets of eyes starting at my naked body.

Show up on time and come prepared, the first rule said.

Check, I said to myself. *Although I'm not sure coming to class with two steel balls embedded in my pussy qualifies exactly as 'prepared'.*

Suddenly, I felt the balls begin to tremble inside me, and I shifted uncomfortably on my chair.

Stay mentally and physically present, the second rule said.

I'm physically present alright, but my *mind* is definitely elsewhere.

I drew my focus back about ten feet, noticing the cute brunette in the front row swinging her legs as she slowly etched her pencil over her drawing pad. In my periphery, I could see the white fringes on the bottom of her shorts flapping over her inner thighs, and I wondered if she was doing it to help focus on her drawing, or if it was because she was getting aroused by my naked body.

I could feel my nipples hardening as I watched her hands moving over the canvas, wondering what it would feel like to have her touch my *real* body. Hannah must have noticed my distraction, because I could feel the movement of the Ben-wa balls steadily increasing inside my pussy. Suddenly, I was mindful of how wet the chrome seat under my ass had become, feeling the tip of my clit dip into the little puddle I'd created in the concave surface of the stool. As she dialed up the vibration of the two balls shaking inside me, the radiating forces on the underside of my vulva made little ripples in the fluid, splashing gently back and forth over my tingling bulb.

Great, I grimaced. *Just what I need right now. Yet another form of uncontrolled stimulation to my most sensitive body part.*

I was tempted to lower my pinky under my resting palms to stimulate my aching clit, then I remembered the purpose of this exercise was to *contain* my pleasure not encourage it.

Contribute to the meeting goals, the third rule on the sign said.

Check, I said, clenching my buttock cheeks to fight off the rising passion.

I adjusted my focus to the pretty redhead in the same line of sight and noticed her cheeks flushing over her pale skin. For a moment, I imagined what it would be like to suck on her pretty pussy while I watched a deeper flush roll over her naked chest.

Get it together Jade, I said to myself, glancing up at the clock on the wall. *You only need to get through another fifteen minutes, then you can fantasize all you want about fucking these cuties.*

My eyes drifted back to the sign above Denzel Washington's head, reading the fourth rule.

Let everyone participate, it instructed.

I peered down a few inches, noticing his arm muscles flexing as he brushed his fingers over his canvas.

I bet he knows how to please a woman with those soft hands of his, I fantasized.

Suddenly I felt the two chrome balls begin to flex back and forth, caressing the walls of my dripping pussy. While they pounded inside me, I imagined his cock sliding in and out of my hole as I gripped his powerful arms.

Fuck, Hannah, I cursed under my breath. It was almost like she was reading my mind, adjusting the action of the Ben-wa balls to mimic the fantasies that were racing through my mind.

With the pleasurable sensations steadily building inside my womb, I could feel my breathing increasing as my breasts began to rise and fall on my chest. Surely everyone must have noticed my internal distraction, and I half expected the teacher to admonish me to remain still. But she was too busy circulating among the group to pay any attention to me. When she angled back toward the front of the room, she bent over to observe the brunette's work, and I gawked at her fleshy breasts, barely supported by the flimsy fabric of her blouse.

God damn, I murmured. *I'd love to bury my face in those tits. Or better yet, rub my cunt against her melons while she watched me squirt all over her body.*

As my body continued to heave unconsciously on my stool, my clit dipped in and out of the increasingly large puddle I was forming on the seat, and I clenched my jaw trying to stifle my rising passion.

I glanced back up at the wall clock and noticed I only had five minutes left to finish my test. Recognizing my increasing distress, Hannah flicked her thumbs over the remote control and suddenly I felt the Ben-was balls begin to *rotate* on their axis.

Oh my God, I panted under my breath. *What else can these evil things do?*

By now, I was being silently fucked by the three-way action of the miniature dumbbells. In addition to flexing back and forth, they were twirling inside me like a slingshot, while rotating rapidly. The combined stimulation on the walls of my pussy was almost unbearable.

I could see my thigh muscles clenching as I stiffened my body trying to fight back the rising wall of pleasure, but just as I was about to pop off, the teacher stood up and told everyone to put their pencils down. Suddenly, the whirring balls stopped moving inside me and I relaxed my buttock muscles, feeling my burning lips dip back down into the warm puddle beneath me.

"Okay everyone," Danielle announced. "Time's up. Please stop sketching and bring your completed compositions to the front of the room before you leave. Jade, you may put on your robe now. Thank you for your time and participation in today's art class. We have a small parting gift for you before you leave. Next week, we have a *sculpture* class scheduled. If you'd like to come back and join us again, we'd love to have you."

I pulled the robe back over my shoulders, then Danielle handed me a long cardboard tube and thanked me again for my participation.

"If you'd like to model for us again, please let me know," she said, clasping my shaking hand. "You seem to have inspired a whole new level of dedication in my students' craft."

Later that day when I got home and opened the tube, I pulled out a long piece of parchment paper. Sketched on the front was a picture of me with my head thrown back in the throes of passion with my hands positioned in front of my snatch between my outspread legs. But instead of the stool I was sitting on in class, I was sitting on a giant, stylized chrome dildo, deeply embedded in my pussy. The signature on the bottom of the sketch simply read *Han*.

I smiled, admiring the surreal illustration.

"I didn't know you could draw, you little devil," I said.

Then I pulled my favorite rabbit vibrator out of my nightstand and rammed it inside me, beginning to dream of what fantasy Hannah had in store for me next.

6

"**I** can't *imagine* what you have planned for this final test," I said to Hannah when she came to pick me up a few days later. "What could be more difficult than having to stand motionless for thirty minutes while you stimulate me completely naked in front of twenty sexy college students?"

"That was pretty hot," Hannah nodded. "You definitely earned your choice of five-star restaurants on our little getaway to Bora Bora."

"What's my motivation for this last challenge?" I said. "Everything's already pretty much paid for. What's stopping me from just enjoying myself and letting it all go?"

"How does a snorkeling expedition to swim with the sharks and rays in the crystalline waters of an off-shore reef sound?"

"Not as dangerous as what I suspect you've got cooked up for me today."

"What about a catamaran cruise to our own private island for a candlelight dinner under the stars?"

"That's definitely on my bucket list..."

"Or a full-day spa treatment with hot stone massage, deep-clean facial, and sensuous body scrub?"

"Okay, *fine*, you little bugger," I chuckled. "You've twisted my arm. So, what have you got in store for me today?"

Hannah paused as her mouth curled up on one side.

"Watching you try to recite the prayers while I stimulated you at the church got me thinking. That was almost too *easy* with everyone looking the other way. At this *next* venue, everyone's going to be hanging on your every word..."

"What–am I going to be giving some kind a speech or something?"

"Almost," she smiled. "You're going to be reading a book for some of my book club friends."

"What's the book?"

"Delta of Venus, by Anais Nin."

"I've heard of that," I nodded. "Isn't that the one with all the steamy vignettes describing the author's sexual escapades?"

"Yes."

"So let me get this straight," I said. "You want me to read a story describing graphic sex without getting aroused while you stimulate me from a distance with a secret vibrator?"

"Exactly."

I shook my head, hardly believing the lengths Hannah had gone to to dream up these outrageous scenarios.

"Who will be my audience?"

"It's an LGBT book club, so it'll be a group of about twenty young women–"

"You've *got* to be kidding me," I said. "You expect me to remain composed while I'm reading a sex scene surrounded by a bunch of hot lesbians?"

"If you want the spa and the cruise and the snorkeling expedition..." she smirked.

"You are *truly* an evil witch, you know that, right?"

"That's why you love me so much," Hannah said, rubbing up against me playfully.

"And where exactly is this latest excursion going to take place?" I said, wondering what else she was planning to raise the stakes.

"At the local bookstore. They have a little coffee shop in the back which they allow our group to use from time to time."

"Great," I said, pushing her away in disgust. "So you're going to be diddling me as an untold number of strangers walk in and out of the coffee shop?"

"Mmm-hmm," Hannah nodded.

"Will you be using Ben-wa balls again, since I'll be exposed to the public?"

"Oh *no*," Hannah said, shaking her head teasingly. "We'll have to make this a little more interesting if you want to pass the ultimate test."

"You've already subjected me to the dual action of the *We-Vibe* vibrator. What could possibly be more stimulating than that?"

Hannah reached into her purse and pulled out a familiar finger-shaped toy.

"Not the *Osé* vibrator!" I squealed. "You're making this almost impossible! How do you expect me to control myself with a realistic finger and tongue caressing my private parts while I'm getting turned on reading a sexy story to a bunch of sexy women?"

"*You're* the one who bragged about how easily you can turn it on and off," Hannah shrugged. "If you pass this final test, I'll give you whatever you want."

"If I pass this test," I said, crossing my arms indignantly, "I'll expect Scarlett Johansson as my personal masseuse and Thomas Keller as our chef!"

"I'll see what I can arrange..."

When we got to the bookstore, Hannah set me up on a comfortable settee with a small reading table. On its surface rested a hardcover book with an image of a half-naked woman kneeling on an upholstered chair with her legs splayed in a sexy pose.

At least I'll be reasonably covered up this time, I thought, beginning to get aroused looking at the provocative picture.

Hannah had allowed me to wear a loose-fitting summer dress that concealed most of my body, but she'd insisted I go au naturel underneath to permit maximum freedom of movement for both me and the vibrator. As the book club members began to wander into the bookstore, she introduced me to each one in turn, and I was struck by how young and pretty they all were. It was far cry from the collection of frumpy nerds I'd half-expected. When everybody had assembled in the lounge, she stood up to address the group while I tried to compose myself by straightening out my dress over my shaking knees.

"Welcome to the monthly meeting of the Literary Coven book group," Hannah said. "Today I've invited a special guest to read a passage from one of my favorite erotic books, Delta of Venus, by Anais Nin. She's kindly, um, *volunteered* to read a chapter I think you'll find quite stimulating and moving. So without any further ado, I give you my friend, Jade."

The women clapped softly while they examined my naked shoulders and legs as I smiled back at them politely. I shifted my weight to the edge of the settee and picked up the book, turning to the bookmarked chapter, titled *Elena*.

The three women met, I read softly, *driven inside the same cafe on a day of heavy rain...*

I had no idea when Hannah would begin her private stimulation of me and the anticipation made the reading all the more tension-filled.

Leila, perfumed and dashing, carrying her head high, a silver fox stole undulating around her shoulders over her trim black suit...

What beautiful prose, I thought to myself, already beginning to lose myself in the story.

Elena, in a wine-colored velvet, and Bijou, in her streetwalker's costume, which she could never abandon, the tight-fitting black dress and high-heeled shoes.

Interesting premise, I said to myself. I was already hooked, beginning to understand the attraction of sharing a well-written book with a collection of like-minded women. I glanced over at Hannah, who was peering at me with a devilish look in her eyes.

Suddenly, I felt the long finger of the Osé vibrator beginning to flex inside my pussy, and I squirmed on my seat trying to distract myself from the humanlike sensation.

Leila smiled at Bijou, I said, pausing to collect my breath, *then recognized Elena. Shivering, the three of them sat down before aperitifs.*

As I continued reading the story, Hannah slowly ramped up the vibration of the undulating finger caressing the walls of my pussy while I struggled to maintain my composure.

What Elena had not expected, I shuddered, *was to be completely intoxicated with Bijou's voluptuous charm. On her right sat Leila, incisive, brilliant, and on her left, Bijou, like a bed of sensuality Elena wanted to fall into.*

While I read the exquisitely written book, I found myself getting increasingly pulled into the story, imagining myself in the role of Elena, surrounded by the two fascinating women. When the story took a sexy turn, I found my body reacting as if I were right there with them.

The first one to move was Leila, I read, looking up to see a pretty blonde staring squarely into my eyes. *Who slid her jeweled hand under Bijou's skirt and gasped slightly with surprise at the unexpected touch of flesh where she had expected to find silky underwear.*

I paused for a moment to take a drink of water. The group nodded at me softly, recognizing my silent torment.

Leila had a moment of jealousy, I read, gulping down the last bit of water in my mouth. *Each caress she gave to Bijou, Bijou transmitted to Elena—the very same caress.*

I jerked suddenly in my seat and closed my eyes, feeling the pleasurable sensations from the undulating wand beginning to wash over me.

"Sorry," I said, looking up. "I guess I'm getting more attached to this story than I expected."

"Don't worry," one of the girls whispered. "We're enjoying your rendition. We've never had someone read a book so...*passionately*."

I peered over at Hannah, who was looking at me with a wicked grin. I cleared my throat, feeling the lips of my vulva moistening with a light dew.

After Leila kissed Bijou's luxuriant mouth, I read, turning the page, *Bijou took Elena's lips between her own. When Leila's hand slipped further under Bijou's dress*–huh! I gasped, feeling a wave of pleasure roll over me–*Bijou slid her hand under Elena's. Elena, seeing Bijou offered, dared to touch her voluptuous body, following every contour of her rich curves...*

As I continued reading the erotic story, my hips began to move unconsciously on the dimpled settee, mimicking the action of the characters in the story. I could feel the moisture beginning to pour out of me as the pendulous finger probed deep inside my hole. Coffee shop patrons paused briefly to peer over at me, pinching their eyebrows trying to imagine why I was so immersed in the story.

A bed of down, soft, firm flesh without bones, I read haltingly, *smelling of sandalwood and musk. Her own nipples hardened as she touched Bijou's breasts.*

Suddenly I became aware of how the *rest* of my body was responding as I read the sexy tale. With my bare nipples rubbing against the soft cotton fabric of my dress, every hair on my body was standing on end, as goose bumps covered every square inch of my skin.

When her hand passed around Bijou's buttocks–huh, huh, huh, I spasmed quietly on the sofa–*it met Leila's hand.*

At this point I still only had the internal part of the vibrator moving against me, and I shuddered to think how I would keep it together if and when Hannah turned on the other half of the device. As the action in the story continued to ramp up, so did the pleasure continuing to build unabated in my twitching pussy.

Leila began to undress, I panted, *exposing a soft little black satin corselet, which held her stockings with tiny black garters. Her thighs...slender and white, gleamed...her sex lay in shadow.*

Fuck me, I thought, picturing the scene like I was right there. *This is an incredibly erotic story. To hell with reading this in public—as soon as I get home, I'm going to rip off my clothes and enjoy this properly in the privacy of my own bedroom.*

Hannah suddenly peered up at me, reading my thoughts, and I felt the snake-like appendage hidden in the *other* end of the vibrator begin to press up against my burning clit.

Oh God, I panted under my breath, trying to steel myself against the rising passion beginning to consume my body.

Leila pressed Bijou onto her side, I hissed, *with one leg thrown over Leila's shoulder. And she was kissing Bijou between her–uhn–legs.*

While I read the increasingly bawdy scene, my face contorted in a series of pained expressions as I tried to ignore the animatronic appendages caressing both sides of my pussy.

Now and then...Bijou jerked backwards...away from the stinging kisses and bites, the tongue that was as hard as a man's sex.

Hannah must have chosen this passage explicitly, knowing how much it would torture me to read a passage mirroring the action of the device whirring and shaking against my vulva. As I continued reading the story, she modulated the type and intensity of the device's movement to match precisely how the characters were interacting.

With her hands, Elena had been enjoying the shape of Bijou's body, and now she inserted her finger into the tight little aperture...

I groaned out loud, feeling the disembodied finger beginning to caress the front of my G-spot.

There she could feel, I moaned, *every contraction caused by Leila's kisses–uhn–as if she were touching the wall against which Leila moved her tongue.*

As the fleshy tongue of the Osé vibrator rolled over my tingling clit, I felt myself beginning to lose control. The wall of pleasure rising within me was like a riptide, pushing back against my feeble attempt to resist the flow.

When she was about to come and could no longer defend herself against her pleasure–uh, uh, I heaved–Leila stopped kissing her, leaving Bijou halfway on the peak of an excruciating sensation, half-crazed.

Recognizing that I was on the verge of coming, Hannah simultaneously stopped the vibrator, and I looked up at her with a start.

Please, I mouthed to her, asking her to release me from my torment. She held up her finger up and twirled it in circles, instructing me to finish the chapter. I closed my eyes, taking a deep breath, and resumed reading.

Uncontrollable now, I gasped, *like some magnificent maniac, Bijou threw herself over Elena's body, parted her legs, placed herself between them, glued her sex to Elena's and moved, moved with desperation.*

Yes, I whispered softly, desperate to consummate my own pleasure along with my new imaginary friends.

Elena was now in the frenzy before climax, I cackled, feeling both parts of the vibrator starting up inside me again. *She felt a hand under her, a hand she could rub against. She wanted to throw herself on it until it made her come, but she also wanted to prolong her pleasure.*

Hannah turned down the motion of the finger thrusting inside me again, and I cursed her under my breath.

So she ceased moving, but the hand pursued her, I grunted. *She stood up, and the hand again traveled towards her sex...*

Possessed of another spirit, I slowly rose out of my chair, cradling the book in two hands as streams of lubrication trickled down the inside of my thighs below the hem of my dress.

Then she felt Bijou standing against her back, panting. She felt the pointed breasts, the brushing of Bijou's sexual hair against her buttocks.

As I read the captivating text, my *own* body began to sway and undulate against my literary lover.

Bijou rubbed against her, knowing the friction would force Elena to turn so as to feel this on her breasts, sex, and belly. Elena's body was so burning hot that she feared one more touch would set off the explosion. Leila sensed this, and the two of them together attacked Bijou, intent on drawing from her the ultimate sensation.

Fuck yes, I panted out loud.

She was begging now to be satisfied, spread her legs, sought to satisfy herself by friction against the others' bodies. With tongues and fingers, they pried into her, back and front, sometimes stopping to touch each other's tongue–Elena and Leila, mouth to mouth, tongues curled together, over Bijou's spread legs.

"Oh God", I squealed, feeling my climax beginning to overtake me. *Fuck the massage and the snorkeling expedition*, I said to myself. *I need to be taken right now.*

As I read the final passage of the chapter, my hips began to shake while I struggled to hold the book in my hands.

Bijou's orgasm came like an exquisite torment, I read. *At each spasm, she moved as if she were being stabbed.*

Suddenly, the walls of my pussy clamped down hard and I gushed like a waterfall onto the hard wooden floor beneath me. Every one of the book club members gasped, realizing what was happening to me, then silence filled the room as I stood trembling in the throes of the most powerful orgasm I could remember.

When I finally put the book down, I looked up at them meekly. They stared at me for a long moment, still in shock at what they'd just witnessed, then they all stood up, clapping loudly in unison. As I smiled back at them, feeling the cool sticky moisture between my legs, I glanced over at Hannah and she nodded toward me, joining the others in applause.

I shook my head in amazement, realizing I'd earned every piece of her promised prize.

VOLUME FIVE

THE SPA

VICTORIA RUSH

1

____

"What's up, girl?" my best friend Hannah said to me at our weekly lunch date. "You look a little run down. Have you been taking care of yourself?"

"I've been going to yoga class as often as I can, and I think I'm eating reasonably well. But I've kind of been flitting from one empty relationship to another, and I guess I'm in a bit of a rut."

"Mmm," Hannah nodded. "Maybe you need to break away from your routine for a change. You know, mix up the scenery, go somewhere you can relax and recharge your batteries."

"What did you have in mind?" I said.

"I've been thinking," she smiled with a slight curl of her lip. "I've heard about this new spa in town that takes a different slant on the whole wellness concept."

"How so?"

"Well, for one thing, it's for ladies only."

"That's nothing new. Ninety-five percent of the clientele at most spas is already women."

"This one's on the top floor of one of the tallest skyscrapers in Chicago. It's got a retractable roof and a beautiful open-air patio surrounding a huge pool with magnificent views of the city and the lake."

"That *does* sound a little more upscale than most," I nodded. "But if that's its big claim to fame, I'm not sure that's going to be enough to pull me out of my funk."

"What if I told you it's a *naked* spa?"

"What do you mean?" I said, suddenly intrigued. "You mean customers receive facials and massages in the nude?"

"Well yes, but it's much more than that. I mean *everybody's* naked, including in the common areas like the pool, sauna, and exercise studio."

"Really? Like a nudist camp or something?"

"A very *elite* nudist camp," she smiled. "With all the spa amenities. Where everybody is super wellness-oriented and in fabulous shape. Imagine sitting poolside watching all the hot women going in and out of the pool and cavorting in the hot tub."

I shifted unsteadily on my chair, suddenly realizing how wet my panties had become envisioning the scenario.

"Is there a *lot* of cavorting going on?"

"Let's just say it's a voyeur's paradise, where women are encouraged to mingle. From what I've heard, it's Chicago's answer to Plato's Retreat. There's allegedly a ton of extra-curricular activities going on. Don't tell me that doesn't get your juices going."

"Um–*yeah*," I said, feeling my pussy throb at the idea of an all-girls venue. "That does sound a little different. What about the staff? They don't have a problem with all that lewd socializing?"

"Quite the opposite. Apparently, they're just as involved in the delivery of the special services. Can you imagine getting a full-body massage with a hot masseuse with all the extra benefits? Or a Brazilian, or a pedicure, or a facial where they make sure you're satisfied in *every* possible way?"

I leaned back in my chair, scrunching up my face.

"Don't you think it would be kind of weird getting a wax where the aesthetician is focused on more than just cleaning things up down there?"

"You never know until you try," Hannah said. "Come on, Jade–you deserve to be pampered for a change. This is a place you can go where there's no judging, no expectations, no relationship pressures. You can indulge as little or as much as you wish in the carnal opportunities. Or just lie in the sun, go for a dip in the pool, and take in the scenery."

"The very *erotic* scenery," I smiled.

"That never stopped you before," she said, arching an eyebrow.

"Okay," I said. "You've twisted my arm. When did you have in mind for this little excursion?"

"Tomorrow at noon," she said, holding up two tickets. "I've already paid for both of us. My treat."

"Are you planning to be my wingwoman to keep me out of trouble?"

"Fuck *that*," Hannah chuckled. "I'm going to be your *partner-in-crime*, to make sure you get into as much trouble as possible."

2

———

The following day, I met Hannah in the lobby of an office tower on Magnificent Mile. It was a beautiful sunny day, and I could see all the way down Grand Avenue toward the Navy Pier and Lake Michigan. I was ready to forget my troubles and lose myself in the luxury and decadence of the upscale spa. I had no idea what I was in for, but the throbbing in my pussy suggested it would be anything but boring.

"So, are you ready for this?" Hannah said while we waited for the elevator on the ground floor.

"I think so," I said. "My *mind* isn't so sure, but my body seems to have other ideas."

We stepped into the lift and Hannah nodded, tapping the button for the sixty-third floor.

"I'm just as excited as you are to see what this is all about. My mind's been racing with all the possibilities ever since I bought the tickets."

"You had this planned for me all along, didn't you?" I said.

"Of course," Hannah smirked. "How could I not invite my bestie to the hottest show in town?"

When the elevator reached the top floor and the doors opened, I saw a pretty attendant dressed in a blue uniform sitting behind a frosted-glass desk flanked by a streaming water wall.

"It's impressive looking, that's for sure," I said. "But I thought you said all the staff were naked?"

"They have to present a professional face to the general public," Hannah said. "But I assure you, once we get behind the reception area, it will be an entirely different picture. Come on, let's check this place out."

We strolled up to the front counter, and the attendant looked up from her computer screen.

"Good afternoon," the girl said. "How can I be of service?"

"We have two day-passes," Hannah said, sliding the tickets over the counter.

"Of course," the girl said, peering at the tickets. "You're welcome to use all of our club's features at your leisure. There's the pool of course, the outdoor patio, the hot tub, sauna, and exercise studio. But if you wish to avail yourselves of the special services, you'll have to make an appointment."

"What services do you offer, specifically?"

"Our aestheticians and massage therapists provide facials, mani-cures/pedicures, massages, and intimate grooming."

Hannah turned toward me and smiled.

"What do you think, Jade? What would you like to do first?"

"I think I'm pretty good with the grooming. How about a massage?"

I looked toward the attendant.

"Do you offer doubles massages? When's your next opening?"

"We do," she said. "Our therapists are just finishing up with another appointment. They should be available in about twenty minutes if you'd both like to give it a try."

"Yes, thank you," Hannah nodded.

The attendant handed each of us a card key to enter the premises and separate locker keys.

"The change room is through the door to the left. Each of the service areas is clearly marked. The massage therapists will be waiting for you at one p.m."

"Is there a particular dress code while traveling about the common areas?" Hannah asked.

"You'll find a terrycloth robe in each of your lockers and two large bath towels. You're welcome to wear either of these in the common areas or nothing at all, if you prefer. We want you to feel as relaxed and comfortable as possible at all times. Most of our guests choose to relax in the nude, as they find that most liberating."

Liberating, indeed, I smiled at the attendant, noticing a gleam in her eye.

Hannah and I took our keys and passed through the locked guest door, then followed the signs to the change room. When we got there, there was a handful of women coming in and out of the showers, making little effort to conceal their naked bodies. Most of them looked to be in their twenties and early thirties, with well-toned figures and golden-brown skin.

"Looks like we're going be the old ladies of the bunch," Hannah chuckled, opening her locker next to mine.

"I'm okay with that," I said, taking off my clothes and hanging them in the locker next to the robe. "If this is any indication of what the rest of the customers look like, that'll work for me. Besides, we're no slouches. I think we can hold our own against the competition."

Hannah peered at a pretty blonde giving her the eye as she bent over to step out of her pants.

"Something tells me there's going to be a *lot* of holding our own against these ladies before the day is over," she winked.

I glanced at a slim African-American girl emerging from one of the showers. She had flawless caramel-colored skin and a model-perfect figure with firm, high breasts, a narrow waist, and an exquis-itely rounded ass. As she patted her short afro dry, I stole a glance between her legs, watching the water drip down over her bald, brown mound.

"Jesus," I said. "I could jump any one of these girls right now. I hope these ladies are just getting *started* their spa treatment, not finishing."

"Not to worry," Hannah smiled, noticing me drooling at the pretty black girl. "I'm pretty sure there's lots more where those came from. Just try to keep your dick in your pants for a little longer while we ease our way into this experience."

"Whatever you say, boss," I said. "So what's the protocol? Do we wear our robes into the massage room or traipse around in the buff like everyone else it seems to be doing?"

"I don't see any harm in wearing the robe to start," Hannah said. "Besides, we need *somewhere* we store our locker keys."

"Come on," she said, glancing at her phone screen before placing it on the locker shelf and locking the door. "It's time for our massage."

I followed Hannah down the hall to the waiting area for the massages, where we sat in the plush chairs, picking up two copies of Vogue magazine lying on the adjacent tables. As I began leafing through the glamour shots of the gorgeous models, I wondered how many of them had frequented this place. The African-American girl I saw in the change room certainly could have qualified for any of these shoots, and I felt my nipples hardening at the idea of engaging with her later. After a few minutes, the door to the massage room opened and a nude brunette girl approached us.

She had a more athletic figure than the black girl from the locker room, but was equally stunning. With large, round tits and a perfectly toned stomach and bare midriff, my pussy began watering just looking at her.

"Are you Hannah and Jade for the one o'clock massage appointment?"

"Um, yes," I stammered, momentarily taken aback by her casual attitude and Amazonesque figure.

"Please," she said. "Come in."

When we entered the room, I saw a second attendant leaning over a sink washing her hands as her tight ass flexed over rippling hamstrings and calves. I looked at Hannah with wide eyes, mouthing the words *Holy Shit!* She peered back at me with an equally incredulous look, shrugging her shoulders.

"Just go with the flow, baby," she whispered.

In the middle of the room rested two side-by-side massage tables about four feet apart, covered with a long bath sheet and a rolled-up towel resting in the middle section.

"Can we hang your robes for you?" the brunette said as the blonde attendant turned around, drying her hands.

She was even more beautiful than the brunette, with long silky hair tied up in a bun and a slender figure with the most exquisite tits I'd seen in a long time. With her compact round ass, long slender legs, and mouth-wateringly curvy hips, she had the figure of a twenty-year-old stripper. I could feel the moisture rapidly building up between my legs as a trickle of lubrication dripped down the inside of my thigh.

"By all means," Hannah said, practically throwing her robe at the attendant.

"Make yourselves comfortable on the massage tables, facing face-down," the brunette said, obviously the more experienced of the two girls.

When I lay down on one of the benches, I was happy when I saw the blonde girl approach my table with a bottle of massage oil. I would have been happy to have either girl touch me, but there was something about the blonde one that got my juices flowing. As I watched the brunette hovering over Hannah's naked body pouring oil into her hands, I glanced at Hannah with wide eyes. Neither of us had to say a word, since both of us were thinking the same thing. This was as close to heaven as two living and breathing people surely could have gotten.

When I felt the blonde's slippery hands run up my spine starting from the small of my back, at first I flinched from the unexpected sensation. But after she began softly pressing her thumbs and fingers into my muscles, I slowly relaxed, flitting my eyes in sublime bliss. Normally, I closed my eyes when I got a massage, concentrating on the relaxing feeling of my masseuse's fingers kneading my body. But with Hannah lying right next to me being serviced by a gorgeous Amazon, I kept them wide open, following her every movement and muscle twitch.

As she pressed her fingers into Hannah's back and slid her hands up and down her spine, I watched her tits jiggling and the muscles in her arms and stomach flexing. Her lower body was partially obscured by Hannah's prone figure, but that didn't stop me from dreaming about slipping my fingers into her bare snatch and licking her like a puppy dog. When the girls moved around to opposite sides of our tables revealing their bare asses for both of us to see, Hannah and I looked at one another again with wide eyes.

As I watched the front of my masseuse's body tensing and flexing only inches away from me, it took every ounce of my willpower not to reach out from the side of my table and touch her bald pussy. The more she caressed me, the more worked up I got watching the two girls' asses wiggling mere inches apart, and my hips began to squirm atop the rolled towel pressing into my pubis.

Just when I thought I couldn't take it any longer, the two masseuses moved to the other end of our bodies and began pressing their fingers into our calves, slowly working their way up our legs along the insides of our thighs. When the blonde girl reached the base of my buttocks, she stopped just short of my dripping slit then rolled her hands over my buttocks, squeezing them firmly. I pressed my mound down hard on the bumpy towel, desperately trying to give my aching clit some direct friction.

Feeling my buttocks flexing in her hands and sensing my rising tension, she swept her hands around the sides of my ass, cupping my cheeks with her thumbs pointed toward my fluttering pussy. I spread my legs further apart, inviting her to move her hand closer, and I gasped when she began running her thumbs up and down the sides of my slippery folds.

God yes, I thought, feeling my heart beginning to pound in my chest. *That's where I need your touch right now.*

I glanced over at Hannah, who had an equally intense look on her face as her attendant leaned over, caressing her vulva. I could see the slit of her masseuse's pussy between her round globes, and my eyes darted back and forth between the view of the blonde's bare mound moving inches away from my face and the brunette's inviting pussy glistening in the bright light of the massage room on the other side of Hannah's table.

I peered over at Hannah with my mouth agape and whispered *Thank You*. She simply smiled back at me and nodded knowingly. Something told me she knew exactly what she'd gotten us into, but at this precise moment I couldn't care less about her devious plan. Suddenly, the blonde girl adjusted her position with her left hand rested atop the base of my spine, while her other hand curled under my cheeks, penetrating my hole. When I felt her fingers enter my tunnel, I groaned, tilting my ass higher in the air.

Now I knew what the rolled-up towel was intended for. It was obviously meant to give the masseuses easier access to our undercarriage for this express purpose. As I began to roll my hips in concert with the blonde's probing of my pussy, I felt a stream of oil drip onto my buttocks, flowing down the crack of my ass over my rosebud and her dripping hand, now firmly embedded in my cunt. When I felt her other hand slide down over my ass and begin to massage my pucker, I groaned loudly and closed my eyes.

I was no longer interested in seeing what the other girl was doing to Hannah. I just wanted to concentrate on the heavenly sensation being administered by my own masseuse. When she began flicking my clit with the two little fingers of her right hand while she stimulated the walls of my pussy with her other fingers, I couldn't contain my pleasure any longer.

"Oh God," I moaned, fucking her hands with my ass and my pussy. My entire perineum from my asshole down to my clit was being simultaneously stimulated by the most sexy woman I'd seen in a long time.

"Yes," I purred, opening my eyes to see Hannah equally glazed over as her masseuse ministered to her in a similar manner.

I wondered if the couples' massage was designed to provide each of us simultaneous attention so we could arc through our pleasure in tandem. But at this point I hardly cared, as I surrendered to the mounting pleasure building inside me. Hannah and I peered at each other's faces while we read our bodies, knowing exactly what was happening to each other as we watched our reactions. We raised our arms over our heads and gripped the top of our padded tables tightly with our hands, and our mouths began to gape open as a flush rolled over each of our cheeks.

"Oh fuck," I groaned, feeling my orgasm beginning to pulse through me as my whole body began to shake. As I began clamping down on the blonde's fingers inside my pussy, she slipped her oiled thumb into my pucker while she fucked both of my holes as I writhed in delirious pleasure on the massage table.

"Uhnnn," Hannah groaned as I watched her ass quivering in the throes of her own powerful climax. The sight of the two gorgeous masseuse's fucking us with both hands while their bodies tensed and writhed overtop of our prone bodies was the most erotic thing I'd experienced in ages.

Hannah and I trembled and moaned on the massage tables for what seemed like an eternity, then our bodies both fell limp as our climaxes receded. For the first time in a long time, I felt completely relaxed and satisfied.

Maybe this spa idea wasn't such a bad idea after all, I smiled toward Hannah lying on the table next to me.

After Hannah and I recovered from our dual massages, we headed to the pool to relax. The view of the city from the rooftop patio was magnificent, but the view *inside* was even more heart-stopping. Scores of naked women paraded in and out of the pool, while another group giggled inside an oversize, bubbling Jacuzzi. With the glass roof retracted, the bright overhead sun reflected off their glistening skin like sequins on their bare bodies.

We found two lounge chairs facing the shallow end of the pool and lay our bath towels on the padded cushions, then propped up the seatbacks so we'd have a good view of the action. The shallow end had descending steps leading into the basin, so we had a front-row seat for viewing the women as they slunk in and out of the water. As I watched the procession of beauties emerging from the pool dripping in erotic sensuality, I squeezed my thighs together trying to quiet my burning clit.

"You weren't kidding about this place being a voyeur's paradise," I chuckled to Hannah.

"Tell me about it," she said. "I can't decide if I prefer them coming or going."

"I could come again watching them either way. Is *everybody* in this place drop-dead gorgeous with model-perfect figures?"

"Well, it *is* the city's most exclusive spa, so I guess these girls know how to take care of themselves. But I also suspect a lot of it has to do with the fact that they know they're going to be under a microscope traipsing around in the nude. Maybe only the prettiest ones feel confident enough to flaunt their bodies so openly."

"Don't get me wrong," I said. "I'm definitely enjoying the show. It's just that I haven't felt this self-conscious about my body in a long time."

Hannah cocked her head toward me, peering over the top of her sunglasses.

"Don't sell yourself short, girl. You're just as pretty and sexy as any one of these hot mamas. Maybe you should get out there and do a little flaunting of your own."

"Perhaps in a little while," I said. "Right now, I'm just happy to do the watching."

"So are you glad I twisted your arm to come up here?" she said, lying back in her chair to soak up the sun.

"Definitely. This is even more dreamy than I imagined."

"And did you enjoy your massage?"

"Couldn't you tell? I think my masseuse probed every one of my erogenous zones."

"That's what I call a *full-body* massage," Hannah smiled.

"I was kind of hoping they'd flip us over afterward and get on top of us to complete the procedure. I don't know about you, but I had a hard time resisting the temptation to reach out and grope them as they moved around the table."

"I suspect that was all by design," Hannah nodded. "To build up our excitement for the big finish."

"That was a hell of a happy ending. I haven't come that hard in months."

"And we're just getting started," Hannah smiled. "Think of all the opportunities to connect in this place."

Suddenly, I noticed the pretty black girl from the locker room emerge from the outside patio and begin to walk in our direction.

"Oh, I'm *thinking*, alright," I said, pushing myself higher in my chair to get a better view.

Hannah followed my line of sight toward the girl and smiled.

"Isn't that the same girl you were eyeballing in the change room? She seems to be just as interested in you as you were in her."

As she moved closer toward us, we made eye contact, checking each other's figures out.

"I dunno, Han," I said. "I think she's out of my league. She looks like an African goddess."

"Well it appears that she's going to give us a bird's-eye view of her figure at least. Maybe she'll take a dip in the pool, where we can get a closer look at her."

As the girl walked toward the shallow end of the pool, I watched her tits jiggling on her chest and her long leg muscles flexing. When she got within a few feet of us, she turned toward the turquoise water and paused at the top of the steps. Her backside was even more spectacular than her front, with her swelling hips and a perfectly round ass accentuating her tawny, hourglass figure.

"Fuck me," I whispered to Hannah, peering down the crack of her ass toward the dark folds showing between her slightly parted thighs.

"That could be arranged if you play your cards right," she chuckled.

After a few seconds, the girl stepped into the water, slowly immersing her body into the sparkling surf. Then she leaned forward and began swimming toward the other end using a graceful breast stroke. As her legs flapped in and out, I watched her sexy ass rising and falling under the surface while the water swirled over her caramel body.

"Oh my God," I panted. "*Pinch* me to make sure I'm not dreaming."

"It's not a dream, babe," Hannah smiled. "That is one sexy-ass, flesh-and-blood woman."

"Just when I thought it couldn't possibly get any hotter than those two masseuses that worked us over. I'd take *this* one over three of them in a heartbeat."

When the girl reached the other end of the pool, she flipped over onto her other side and began swimming with a backstroke toward us. While her arms slowly windmilled through the water, her body rolled from side to side as the water washed over her sensuous breasts like waves on a beach. The closer she got to me, the more my heart raced, imagining her swimming right into my moistening lap.

"Yes, sweetheart," I purred, spreading my legs apart. "Dock yourself right here."

Hannah and I sat mesmerized watching her sylphlike figure slicing through the water, until one of her hands tapped the steps in the shallow end. Then she turned around and walked out of the water directly in front of us, smiling as she made eye contact with me. I couldn't help running my eyes over the front of her dripping body as my legs twitched involuntarily. Then she turned and retraced her steps around the perimeter of the pool, reclining in a vacant lounge chair at the opposite end.

"Did you see how she looked at you?" Hannah said, peering over at me. "She was practically fucking you with her eyes."

"I hardly noticed, watching the rest of her incredible body."

"I think you need to take advantage of this opportunity while the iron is still hot," she said. "Why don't you go over there and introduce yourself?"

"I wouldn't exactly say that was a green light to go hit on her. I don't want to intrude on her privacy if she just wants some peace and quiet."

"Well then, why don't you give her some of her own medicine by parading your body up and down the pool for everyone else to see? Let's see if she takes the bait."

"I don't know if *bait* is the right metaphor in this case, but I'd be thrilled if she gobbled me up right about now. I could use a refreshing dip in the pool anyways. After that hot massage session and watching that nymph take a sexy bath, I need to cool off. Hold my chair for me?"

"I wouldn't dream of giving it away. You go girl, go get your Lorelei."

I raised myself up from my chair then walked up to the edge of the shallow end and paused, peering across the reflecting surface hoping to catch the girl watching me from the other end of the pool. Although I was a little more full-figured than her, I maintained a tight, yoga-toned physique, with full, perky breasts, a flat stomach, and curvy hips. My pussy throbbed at the thought of her ogling me as I had with her.

While I lowered myself into the water, I kept my gaze pointed down, pretending to ignore her. Mimicking her lead, I began swimming breast strokes in her direction, with my head bobbing in and out of the water. When I neared the far wall, I glanced up at her chair resting near the edge of the pool and noticed her legs were slightly parted and she had a sexy smile on her face.

Jesus, I thought, touching the wall right in front of her. *Was she signaling her interest in me the same way I had earlier?*

As I turned around, I couldn't help smiling at our sexy cat-and-mouse game, then I pushed back from the wall floating on my back, using a reverse breast stroke technique. While I flapped my legs slowly in and out, I lifted my ass to the surface of the water, letting her watch the churning surf rising and falling over my exposed bare pussy. As I swung my arms slowly behind me, I glanced at the side of the pool and noticed that all the women were staring at my breasts poking out of the water.

Good, I thought. *Maybe if the African-American girl sees that I'm attracting the attention of some of the other pretty women, she'll make the next move.*

When I reached the shallow end, I walked up the stairs slowly so the girl on the other end could watch my round ass dripping with moisture. Then I lay down on my lounge chair next to Hannah, not even bothering to dry off.

"Holy shit, girl," she said. "I think you might have just one-upped your African goddess. Every set of eyes in the room was watching you as you swam across both lengths of the pool. You even got *me* going with that performance. If that doesn't pull her toward you like a magnet, I don't know what will."

I turned my head to gaze in the black girl's direction and noticed she was walking back toward our end once again.

"See?" Hannah said. "You've obviously tweaked her interest. Let's see if she says hello."

As the girl moved closer toward us, I could feel my pussy throbbing, but when she reached the end of the pool, she glimpsed at me briefly then continued on to the end of the platform, disappearing into the sauna room.

"*Well?*" Hannah said, peering at me with raised eyebrows. "What are you waiting for? That's an invitation if I ever saw one."

"Yeah?" I said, still not convinced. "Are you sure?"

"She was watching you the entire walk back toward our end of the pool. Then she goes into a private room in full view of you. I don't think you need a crystal ball to know that she wants you."

"Okay," I said. "Should I bring a towel or something to cover up?"

"Was *she* wearing a towel?" Hannah said sarcastically.

"Fine. But if I'm not out in twenty minutes, come check up on me to make sure I haven't passed out or something. I'm feeling so lightheaded right now, I'm afraid all that hot steam might make me collapse at the knees."

"I'm quite sure you won't need any help from me," she said. "But if she happens to come out first and I don't see any sign of you within a few minutes, I'll make sure you haven't fainted from all the pleasure you're about to receive."

"Wish me luck," I said, slowly rising from my chair, trying not to make it too obvious to everybody else in the room that I was following the girl into the sauna.

When I got to the room, I swung open the door and saw her sitting on the upper bunk with her left knee propped up on the bench, exposing her pink slit. Another woman rested on the bench directly beneath her, leaning back against the wood planks with her hands resting by her sides. I took a position kitty-corner to them on the lower bench, then leaned back against the wall with my opposite leg propped up, concealing my pussy.

I lay my head back and closed my eyes, pretending to relax and enjoy the hot steam. But when I opened them briefly and peered in the black girl's direction, I saw her right hand positioned in front of her pussy, moving her fingers in slow circles below her mound.

Holy shit, I thought. *She's playing with herself in full view of me!*

At first, I was so shocked at her brazen act of exhibitionism that I looked away, thinking she wanted to watch me only when she knew I wasn't looking. But when I peered back at her a few moments later, her legs were spread even further apart, exposing her beautiful pink vulva against her chocolate-brown skin. As her hand began to move in faster circles over her clit, her mouth parted open and I could hear her panting softly.

I glanced down at the other woman sitting below her who still had her eyes closed, oblivious to the ministrations of the sexy girl sitting directly above her. Feeling the sticky juices building up between my legs, I lowered my right hand into my lap and began rubbing my clit behind my propped-up leg. I didn't feel comfortable exposing myself fully in case the other woman opened her eyes, but I gazed directly back at the black girl as we massaged our clits.

As I began to feel the sweat dripping over my forehead and the pleasure spreading throughout my body, I slowly lowered my raised leg and spread my thighs apart, showing the girl my dripping pussy. She grabbed one of her tits with her free hand and pinched her long nipple while she stared at my glistening snatch. Before long, both of us were moaning softly, jilling ourselves with increasing fervor.

When I glanced down at the other woman to make sure it was still safe, I was surprised to see that she also had her legs spread apart and was rubbing her pussy as she watched me playing with myself. But at this point, I was too far gone to stop what I was doing, and knowing that the we were all aligned with our intentions, I began to moan and twist my hips on the warm cedar bench. When the black girl thrust her hand inside her pink folds and began thumping her back against the wall in rising pleasure, I couldn't resist the temptation any longer.

I rose from my bench and walked directly in front of her, positioning my head between her legs, then I pulled her hips hard into my face, eating her pussy like it was my last meal. She placed her hands behind my head and pulled me toward her, squeezing my head between her powerful thighs. As I reached up to grab her tits, I felt the woman's hand from below probing my slit, then she placed two fingers thrust inside me. While I moaned into the black girl's cunt, I lifted one foot and placed it on the bench beside the other woman and I felt her lips suck my erect clit into her mouth.

With my face buried in the black girl's snatch and my own pussy being serviced from below, I moaned into her cleft, feeling my orgasm approaching like a freight train. When it slammed into me, I groaned loudly into the girl's pussy, and she grabbed my hair while she clamped her thighs tightly against the sides of my head, quivering on the edge of the bench.

She held me in this clenched position for so long I was afraid she might suffocate me, but I dared not come up for air while she was in the throes of a powerful orgasm. After many long seconds, she finally loosened her grip and relaxed her legs then she leaned forward, thrusting her tongue into my dripping mouth. As we kissed each other passionately, the woman below removed her fingers from my pussy and I heard the sound of her breathing beginning to escalate while she attended to her own needs.

For the entire time the three of us were in the sauna, none of us had said a single word to one another. I didn't even know the *name* of the girl whose cunt I'd just finished eating out. There was something about this anonymous, no-strings-attached, down-and-dirty spa that I was digging. It didn't look like Hannah would have to save me after all.

For the first time since entering the spa, I felt completely liberated, ready to explore all the carnal opportunities on my own.

4

―――――――

Feeling a bit awkward after my fling in the sauna, I left the room soon after and headed back over to my spot by the pool. I saw Hannah taking a leisurely swim, so I headed over to the juice bar and picked up two smoothies. When I returned to my lounge chair, I glanced around the room, soaking up the scene. With so many sexy women prancing around the place, I was surprised more of them weren't hooking up.

Maybe they're just self-conscious about making out in public, I thought. *Or maybe they're waiting for someone to break the ice.*

I glanced over in the direction of the hot tub, noticing a small group of women chatting and laughing in the bubbly froth.

If that's not the perfect place for a little extra-curricular activity, I don't know what is.

Hannah emerged from the pool and walked toward me, wringing out her hair.

"*So?*" she smiled. "How did it go in there? Did you finally get your freak on with your African goddess?"

"It definitely got pretty hot," I nodded.

"Like, almost *pass-out* hot? I'm a little disappointed you didn't call for reinforcements. Try as I might to attract the attention of other women in this place, everybody seems to be ignoring me."

I glanced at Hannah's naked body, admiring her tight, shapely figure. There was no reason she shouldn't be connecting with other girls, and I felt a little guilty for abandoning her.

"Maybe you just need a little extra *lubricant*," I said. "The hot tub in the corner looks like it might be more conducive for some close-quarter mingling. Do you want to give it a go?"

"Sure," Hannah said. "But don't you need a little time to recover? What happened to your girlfriend?"

"It seems she was only interested in one thing," I shrugged. "But I *could* use a little rest."

I pointed to the tall glass resting on the table beside Hannah's chair.

"I brought you a smoothie. Why don't we cool off before jumping back into the fire?"

Hannah patted her hair dry with a towel then lay back in her chair, taking a sip of her smoothie.

"So, have you had your eye on anyone *else* in this place?"

"Not really," I said. "Just about everybody looks seriously fuckable. I wouldn't mind wrapping my legs around that cute blonde masseuse though, if I had a chance. But I'm guessing that's against the rules."

"I dunno. What's good for the goose is good for the gander, in a manner of speaking. Maybe you just need to get her alone someplace."

"Perhaps I can schedule a *one-on-one* massage next time," I said. "I'm pretty sure I could persuade her to participate in a more interac-tive session if I had her all to myself."

"So you're thinking of coming *back*, then?" Hannah smiled. "Have they got you hooked already?"

"It's pretty hard to ignore a place like this," I nodded. "I wonder if they have monthly memberships?"

"The amenities would seem to fit that model. It's almost like more of a *health club*, with a few extra perks. Albeit some pretty fucking *awesome* perks."

"Speaking of," I said, peering over in the direction of the girls in the hot tub. "Are you ready to check out some of those other amenities?"

"Absolutely," she smiled. "If I can't hook up with someone there, at least I should be able to get some *other* kind of stimulation in the Jacuzzi."

We picked up our unfinished smoothies and carried them over toward the hot tub. When we got there, I noticed there were already four women submerged in the bubbling water and I wondered if there'd be enough room for Hannah and me.

"Have you got room for two more?" I asked.

"Absolutely," one of the girls said. "The more the merrier."

The women pressed their bodies closer together, and Hannah and I scooched in next to them. The water was warmer than I expected, but it didn't take long for me to get used to it, especially with the fleshy bodies of the other women rubbing up next to me.

"I haven't seen you guys here before," a forty-something redhead said, smiling at me. "First time visiting our spa?"

"Yes," I said.

"What do you think so far?"

"It's definitely a different kind of experience," I nodded, not yet ready to reveal just how *much* I'd actually enjoyed it.

"Have you availed yourself of any of the special services yet?" she said.

"Hannah and I had a couples massage a little while ago. It was very invigorating."

"Yes, those masseuses really know how to pinpoint the right spots," she smiled. "I'm Amber by the way."

I scanned her pretty face, admiring her piercing green eyes and high cheekbones. Although she was slightly older than most of the other women in the spa, she was equally as stunning, reminding me of the pretty runway model, Angie Everhart.

"Jade," I said. "And this is–"

"Hannah," Amber nodded. "Nice to see some fresh meat in this place, what do you think girls?" She peered around her, nodding at the other women in the tub, roughly her same age. "This is Kat, Anna, and Tammy."

"So are you guys–" I said, wondering if they came here often.

"Old fogies?" Amber laughed. "Yeah, I guess you could say we're regulars. There's more than *one* way to stay young at heart, you know."

"Speaking of," her friend Kat smiled. "We noticed you and that pretty black girl checking each other out earlier. Were you finally able to consummate your little courtship in the sauna?"

"Um..."

"It's okay," Amber chuckled. "We know *everything* that goes on in this place. Why else would we have lifetime memberships?"

I huffed softly, not quite sure how to respond.

"So are you two–?" Amber said, glancing at Hannah.

"No," Hannah said, shaking her head. "We're just good friends."

"That's a shame, because you look like a perfect match. Two pretty girls, one a blonde, the other a brunette. What are you, like barely *thirty*?"

"That's very generous," Hannah chuckled. "Just a little north of that. Maybe this invigorating spa treatment is beginning to work it's wonders already."

"There's a good chance. But you look like you could use a little extra stimulation. While your girlfriend's been improving her circulation in the steam room, you've been left to your own devices. There's a special spot over here where you can have some extra fun if you want."

"Oh?" Hannah said, suddenly perking up.

"I've been sitting right in front of it this whole time. Would you like to give it a try?"

"Sure," Hannah said, happy to have attracted the attention of some other women finally.

"Come," Amber said, standing up in the pool. "Let's switch positions. You come sit over here next to Kat and I'll sit next to your pretty girlfriend."

While Hannah and Amber switched positions, I took a moment to check out Amber's body. She had plump breasts with surprising firmness for her age and well-toned arms with tight, supple skin. Her wet hair draped over her lightly speckled chest and with her flushed cheeks and erect nipples, I found myself unconsciously spreading my legs trying to increase the flow of swirling water over my throbbing pussy.

When Hannah sat in her vacated spot, Kat suddenly reached under the water, pulling her legs forward a few inches, and Hannah's face lit up.

"*Right?*" Amber smiled, pressing her body up next to me. "I told you you'd like it. There's nothing like an invigorating water jet massage directed to the perfect location. Are you feeling more comfortable now?"

"Oh *yes*," Hannah grunted, shifting her hips closer to the pulsating underwater stream. "This is way better than the usual sex toys I'm accustomed to."

"And the best part is there's no *cleanup* required afterward. You can get off and freshen up at the same time."

"Mmm," Hannah moaned, surrendering to the feeling of the powerful spray stimulating her clit.

Suddenly Kat turned her body toward her and reached under the water, caressing her tits.

"Uhnn," Hannah groaned, turning her face toward Kat as they began kissing.

"Now *that's* a beautiful sight, don't you agree, Jade?"

"Absolutely," I hummed. "This is just what Hannah needed."

Amber placed her hand under the water and extended her arm toward my crotch. When she felt my fingers moving softly over my clit, she lowered her hand a few inches lower, thrusting two fingers into my hole. I didn't know what it was about this place, but I didn't seem to mind the members taking these kinds of liberties with my body. Between the swirling water jets pounding against my hips and Amber's sexy body rubbing up against my breasts, I was more than ready to ramp things up.

"That's a nice tight cunny you have," Amber purred. "Shall I continue?"

"Yes please," I moaned, flitting my eyelids in pleasure.

Amber suddenly raised herself off the bench and turned around to face me, straddling my hips and pressing her mound into my stomach.

"Mmm," she purred, pressing her melons against my tits. "You're *soft*, too. Do you like watching your girlfriend getting off under the water?"

"Yes," I panted.

With the four of us now actively engaged with each other, Tammy raised herself off her seat and sat down over Anna's thighs, facing the rest of us. Apparently, nobody except Amber wanted to miss catching the rest of the action in the hot tub while we groped and caressed one another.

Amber reached behind her back with her hand, cupping my trembling hand as I massaged my pussy. Then she placed three fingers inside me, fucking me while I stimulated my clit. She leaned in to kiss me, and I felt her hips tilt as she began rocking her pussy against the top of my mound. The idea of being fucked by this sexy older redhead while she rubbed her big tits against my breasts excited me tremendously, and before long we were tongue-fucking each other as we moaned into each other's mouths.

I peered over at Anna and Tammy, whose eyes were glazed over watching the rest of us as they rubbed their vulvas together with Anna squeezing her friend's tits from behind. Then I glanced over at Hannah and saw that Kat had angled her body toward her with one leg resting over her thigh, trying to get in on the powerful stream now pulsing toward both of their pussies. She smiled at me, nodding at how pleased she was with the turn of events.

With the heat in the hot tub beginning to ramp up, Amber and I began pressing our hips together more vigorously as our moans began rising in pitch in volume, and I could feel myself veering on the precipice, ready to pop off any second. Sensing I was close, Amber pressed her palm harder against my fluttering hand while she stroked my G-spot with her three fingers. Then she pressed her little finger further down my perineum until it rested against my pucker. While she moved her hand in circles overtop of mine, I spread my legs further apart, moaning loudly into her mouth.

"Yes," I grunted, feeling myself falling over the edge. "You're going to make me cum, Amber. *Oh my God–*"

As my orgasm washed over me, Amber pressed her little finger into my rosebud, and my entire perineum began clamping down over her hand.

"Yes, baby," she purred. "Let it go. Come for Momma."

I could feel her press her pussy more forcefully into my stomach as she rocked her hips with greater urgency, gripping my hips with her thighs.

"Uhnnn!" I cried, consumed with pleasure as I watched the other girls reaching their apex at the same time.

When the six of us finally stopping grunting and groaning, I looked around the spa and noticed that virtually everybody else in the poolroom had suddenly paired up, enjoying their own little moment of bliss.

5

———————

After the wild ride in the hot tub, I needed some alone time, so I headed to the exercise studio to stretch and relax. Finding it empty, I walked over to a large padded mat against the far wall and sat down, pulling my hands toward my feet to loosen my leg muscles. The entire room was lined in floor-to-ceiling mirrors, with equal parts dedicated to aerobic classes, weight machines, and stretching. I remembered seeing aerobic classes on the list of services at the front desk, and I smiled at the thought of everybody's boobs bouncing up and down as they went through their paces.

No wonder everyone in this place is so fit and toned, I thought. There weren't many places in the spa where you could avoid being seen or seeing your own naked body from just about any angle. *There's virtually nowhere to hide or cover up.*

As I moved through my usual yoga poses on the mat, I watched myself in the mirror. I was proud of the tight figure I'd been able to maintain over the years, and I smiled seeing the muscles flexing in my arms and legs while I strained to hold the poses. But stretching in the buff was a whole *different* experience, and I felt my nipples hardening and my pussy moistening as I watched my tits and glistening vulva in the glass.

While I held my toes high off the mat balancing on my ass in a split-leg position, suddenly the door swung open and a familiar face entered the room. It was the pretty blonde from the massage room. She glanced at my exposed pussy reflecting in the mirror and smiled when I lowered my feet, closing my legs to protect my modesty.

"Don't stop on my account," she said, taking a position on the mat a few feet to my side. "A woman with your physique shouldn't be afraid to reveal every part of her glorious figure."

"Thanks," I said, leaning forward to rest my breasts on top of my thighs. "I didn't want to be too bold. I already feel exposed enough in this place as it is."

"You shouldn't feel self-conscious in here," she said. "That's the beauty of this spa. It's a place where women can go to free their minds and spirits without feeling judged in any way."

"It seems that's not the *only* thing that gets freed in this place," I smiled, alluding to our intimate session earlier in the day. "I had no idea I'd be releasing my inhibitions in so many different ways."

"*Jade*, isn't it?" she said, pinching her eyebrows together. "I remember you from this morning's massage."

"Yes," I said, blushing softly.

"I'm Julie," she said, reaching out to extend her hand. "We were never properly introduced."

"No, I suppose not," I said, feeling the hairs on my arms standing on end as I touched her for the first time. "I guess we were too preoccupied with other things."

"Mmm," she nodded. "Have you enjoyed your visit to our spa so far?"

"Oh yes," I said. "It's far surpassed my expectations. It's been a feast for the senses in so many ways. So much so that I needed to come in here and wind down for a few moments."

"I know what you mean," Julie said. "I like to come in here to stretch and meditate between appointments. I find it very therapeutic."

I watched her in the mirror as she twisted and contorted her body into increasingly difficult poses.

"How long have you been working here?"

"Only a couple of months. It's nice that the management allows us to use the facilities along with the rest of the members and guests."

As she moved through her stretches and poses, I marveled at her tight, lithesome figure. She was more slender than me, with smaller but firmer breasts and long, sinewy muscles that flexed sensuously as she went through her motions. When she leaned forward and lifted herself off the mat into a crow position, I admired her flexing arm muscles supporting her weight. But when she shifted into an inverted arm balance with her legs curved up over her shoulders, I couldn't help peering between her legs at her exposed slit.

"I always found that pose one of the tougher ones to hold," I said, feeling my pussy growing wetter by the moment.

"The key is to place your arms far enough apart with your legs positioned forward," she said. "Then slowly tilt your weight until you feel yourself balanced on your hands. Why don't you try it with me?"

She dropped her legs to the floor, then placed her hands and feet on the mat in a bent-over pose.

"You start in this position then gradually shift more of your weight over your hands. When you feel like you're supporting most of your weight on your arms, curl your legs forward and raise your feet off the floor."

I followed Julie's lead, panting heavily as I strained my arm muscles trying to support my weight.

"That's it," she nodded, seeing me raise my ass off the floor. "Now cross your ankles in front of your arms to lock yourself into position."

When I finally achieved the position, it felt surprisingly easy to hold the pose with everything held neatly together.

"That's excellent," Julie smiled. "It's not so difficult when you get into the right position, is it?"

"No," I puffed, staring at her pretty tits pressing together in the bent-over pose.

"Do you want to try something a little more challenging?" she asked.

"Okay," I said, feeling the cool air from below flowing over my exposed pussy.

"Keep your weight balanced over your arms, then unlock your ankles and extend your legs straight out in front of you until they're parallel with the floor."

I followed Julie's direction, grunting loudly as I felt the pressure building on my arms.

"Remember to keep your weight shifted forward so you don't fall back."

After a few seconds of struggling, I managed to achieve the pose, albeit with slightly crooked legs.

"That's fantastic, Jade," Julie said, peering at me in the mirror. "Why don't we take it one step further and see if we can shift into the firefly position."

Julie angled her legs higher in the air, tilting her ass toward the floor until her legs were pointed forty-five degrees up in the air, with her entire body balancing on her outstretched arms. With her pussy staring directly in front of me between her splayed legs, it took all of my concentration to stay focused on executing the technique.

"I'll try," I panted, feeling some drops of lubrication falling onto the mat between my legs.

With my legs pointing forward as much as I could, I slowly lowered my hips toward the floor, balancing my suspended weight over my arms until I matched the angle of Julie's upturned legs. I could feel the strain in my hamstrings from my legs pulled back behind my shoulders, and I glanced in the mirror, seeing the reflection of the bright overhead lights reflecting off my glistening, wet pussy.

"You got it, girl!" Julie said, peering between my legs. "How does it feel?"

"Strangely invigorating," I grunted, running my eyes all over Julie's body in front of me. "But this is killing my hamstrings. I think I need to loosen up a bit more before trying some of these more advanced poses."

"Absolutely," she nodded. "You don't want to hurt yourself. Let's give your muscles a rest before you pull something."

I lowered myself onto the mat then placed my hands beside my quivering legs, breathing heavily in and out.

"That was exhilarating," I said, peering over at Julie. "You've obviously got many talents beyond massage therapy."

"It's all part of the mind-body connection," she smiled. "Strength, flexibility, relaxation. It keeps us healthy in many different ways."

I glanced at her perfect tits glistening with sweat, feeling my pussy throbbing in excitement.

"If this is what it takes to achieve your level of fitness, I'm all in. I don't think I've seen another woman with as perfectly toned a figure as yours."

"You're no slouch yourself, Jade. It's just a matter of building up your stamina. Do you want to try some *partnered* stretching to loosen up your muscles a bit more?"

I'd been waiting for a chance to pair up with the pretty masseuse, and when she indicated she was ready to move to a new phase in our routine, I suddenly became aware of the puddle forming on the mat between my legs.

"As long as you promise not to twist me into a pretzel this time."

"No worries," she smiled. "This next one is super simple and far more relaxing. All you have to do is sit on the mat with your legs extended in front of you, with your feet spread apart a few inches. I'll face towards you with our feet touching together, then we can hold hands and gently pull each other forward and back to stretch the back of our leg muscles."

I nodded, imagining myself rocking back and forth with her in whole *different* kind of position.

Julie shifted her body around in front of me, and when she spread her legs and touched her feet to mine, I felt a surge of electricity coursing through me. I had to fight hard to keep my gaze above her neckline as she smiled and reached out her hands toward me.

"Now bend forward one inch at a time while I hold your arms. When you feel the tension in the back of your thighs, breathe deeply and try to relax until you feel the pressure receding."

I was able to bend forward far enough to clasp her hands, and I smiled when she squeezed me gently.

"Now, let me pull you slowly toward me until you feel tightness in your hamstrings again. Stop me when it begins to bind, then breathe slowly in and out until you feel your leg muscles relax."

I did as she instructed, and after a few minutes Julie was able to pull my upper body almost parallel with my legs resting on the floor.

"There you go," she nodded. "Now let's see if we can do the same thing with the adductor muscles on the inside of your thighs. I want you to spread your feet slowly apart as I maintain tension on your arms. You should feel pressure in the muscles on the side of your crotch as you begin to lengthen the tendons on the inside of your legs."

"I definitely feel *something* there," I huffed, watching the slit between Julie's legs open wider and wider the further I pressed my legs apart. She glanced between my thighs, noticing the wet spot on the mat directly in front of me.

"Remember to go slow," she said. "You definitely don't want to pull *this* muscle. This one's pretty important for maintaining sexual health and flexibility."

"You don't have to remind me twice about that one," I smiled. "I definitely don't want to put a damper on that."

"Okay, now lean back and begin to pull *me* forward now. This way we can *both* benefit from this stretch while we pump the blood through our muscles in this area."

"Yes," I purred, pulling her upper body toward me as we pressed our feet further apart. "I feel my circulation improving already."

The more we pulled our bodies toward one another, the further our legs pressed apart, bringing our pussies closer together and our bodies closer to touching. But just as her face moved to within inches of my throbbing snatch, the gym door swung open and two women paused at the entrance, seeing us in the compromising position.

"Do you mind if we join you?" one of the girls said, staring at the glistening reflection of my wet pussy.

"I'm good if you are, Jade," Julie said while I felt her breath inches away from my dripping pussy.

"Of course," I said, not wanting to throw a wet blanket on our fun. "There's lots of room on the mat for more people."

The girls sat down beside us, assuming a similar position.

"That stretch looks interesting," the first one said. "It certainly looks more stimulating than doing it alone."

"It's even more fun to perform it as a *group*," Julie said. "Why don't we form a circle with our feet touching and see if we can stretch and loosen our muscles *together*?"

She shifted her ass back a few inches then spread her legs further apart, inviting the girls into the circle. They positioned themselves next to us, then Julie spread her arm to her side, clasping the hand of the girl next to her. I did the same until we were all holding hands with our legs forty-five degrees apart, touching our feet in a chain-link circle.

"Well now that we're getting to know each other a little better," the first girl said. "I suppose we should introduce ourselves. I'm Taylor and this is Quinn."

"Pleased to meet you," Julie said. "I'm Julie."

"Jade," I said, nodding to each of the girls.

"So how does this work exactly?" Taylor said, glancing down at the juices coating the inside of my thighs.

"Jade and I were pulling each other to stretch our hamstrings and adductor muscles. But in a perfect circle, we'll be maintaining equal pressure between the four of us, so in order to move closer together, let's try spreading our legs further apart."

As we all followed Julie's instructions, our circle slowly began collapsing into a diamond shape.

"That's the idea," Julie said. "Can you girls feel the tension between your legs the closer we get to one another?"

"Yes, and that's not the *only* thing I'm feeling," Quinn said, glancing at our glistening pussies coming closer together.

"When we get close enough to our partners," Julie said, "reach out and clasp her hands, pulling you closer together. As you rock back and forth, you should be able to spread your feet further apart, slowly releasing the tension on the inside of your thighs."

"Mmm," Taylor groaned. "I feel it. How close should we try to get to one another?"

"As close as possible," Julie smiled. "If you can relax your adductors enough, ideally you should be able to touch in the middle."

As the four of us pulled each other closer and closer, spreading our legs further apart, Julie's upper body began to bend over my hips with her tits edging tantalizingly close to my throbbing pussy. I glanced at Taylor and Quinn, whose feet were pressed against the sides of Julie's and mine, and they smiled at each other as they peered between each of their open legs. Before long, both couple's glistening pussies were only inches apart as we pulled our upper bodies closer toward our hardening nipples and parted mouths. When I felt the strands of Julie's hair caress the top of my breasts, I pulled her harder toward me and she encircled one of my teats in her mouth.

"Mmm," I groaned, trying to spread my legs into a one-hundred-and-eighty-degree split, desperate to feel her pussy up against me.

But after a few moments, she began pulling me in the opposite direction. As I leaned forward over her tight abdomen, I licked my tongue up the crease in the center of her stomach until I reached the base of her tits. Then I sucked her medallions into my mouth, circling her nipples with my tongue, and she tilted her hips forward, touching our vulvas. I moaned loudly into her breasts when I felt our juices intermingling, but as soon as our clits touched, she suddenly leaned forward, pressing her body back in my direction.

I was beginning to go crazy with all this reciprocal teasing, wanting to feel Julie's lips against my own as we ground our pussies together. By now, all four of us had our legs spread into a virtual split, with the original circle collapsed into two parallel lines. Growing impatient, I pulled Julie hard toward me until her body rested on top of me, and she began kissing me as we rubbed our tits and vulvas together. This time, there was no desire for either of one of us to separate while we ground our wet pussies together, rubbing our hard clits over one another.

"Fuck yes," I purred into her mouth. "This is insanely hot. Rub your body against me, Julie."

"You've reached the height of your flexibility," she nodded. "Now just try to relax your muscles while you let the rest of your body enjoy the experience."

"Oh yes," I panted. "I'm definitely shifting my concentration to *other* parts of my body."

I peered at Taylor and Quinn out of the corner of my eye and saw that they were similarly commingled, rubbing their pussies and tits against one another with their legs spread wide apart.

"Uhhn," I heard them groan next to Julie and me.

There was something incredibly sexy about the four of us touching our feet together while we rubbed our bodies next to one another, listening to the mounting passion generated between the four of us. I tilted my head up a few inches and looked in the mirror in front of us. With Julie's legs splayed wide apart and our mounds joined together, I saw both of our slits spread open as our juices rolled down over each other's vulvas. I'd never seen anything so sexy in all my life, and the fact that we were engaged in a two-way affair with Taylor and Quinn right next to us just added to my excitement.

I began to feel the pleasure rising inside me and with our hands no longer needed to pull ourselves together, I wrapped my arms around Julie's back and thrust my tongue into her mouth, feeling my climax edging closer. When it finally hit me, I groaned loudly in Julie's mouth, spraying my juices over her vulva and ass while she grunted simultaneously inside my mouth. As the four of us writhed and groaned on the mat in simultaneous union, I heard some movement by the door and glanced up to see a large group of women pausing at the entrance, with their mouths wide agape.

It didn't take long for them to rush toward us joining us on the mat, rolling together in a giant heap of naked, writing bodies. As we intertwined our arms and legs, sucking and rocking against whatever body part presented itself to each of us, I smiled realizing I'd reached a new kind of nirvana. Something told me this spa was about to become my new go-to gym for the foreseeable future.

MORE EROTICA THEMED BUNDLES BY VICTORIA RUSH:

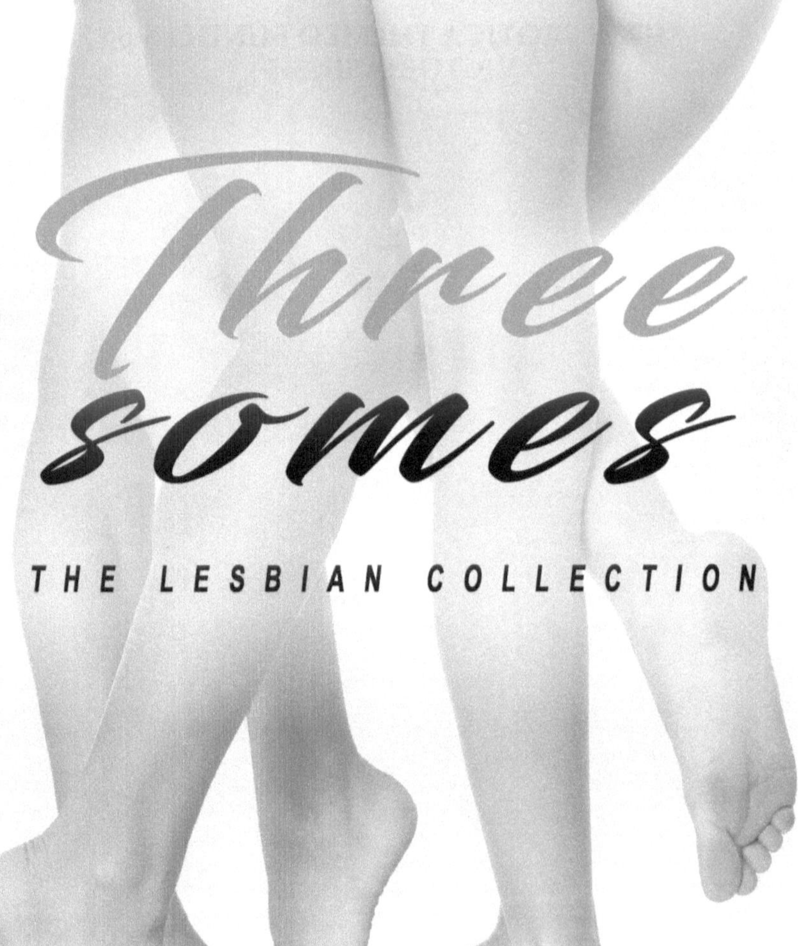

Three
somes
THE LESBIAN COLLECTION
VICTORIA RUSH
2 + 1 = a hundred ways to have fun...

FUTA

Fantasies

THE LADYBOY COLLECTION

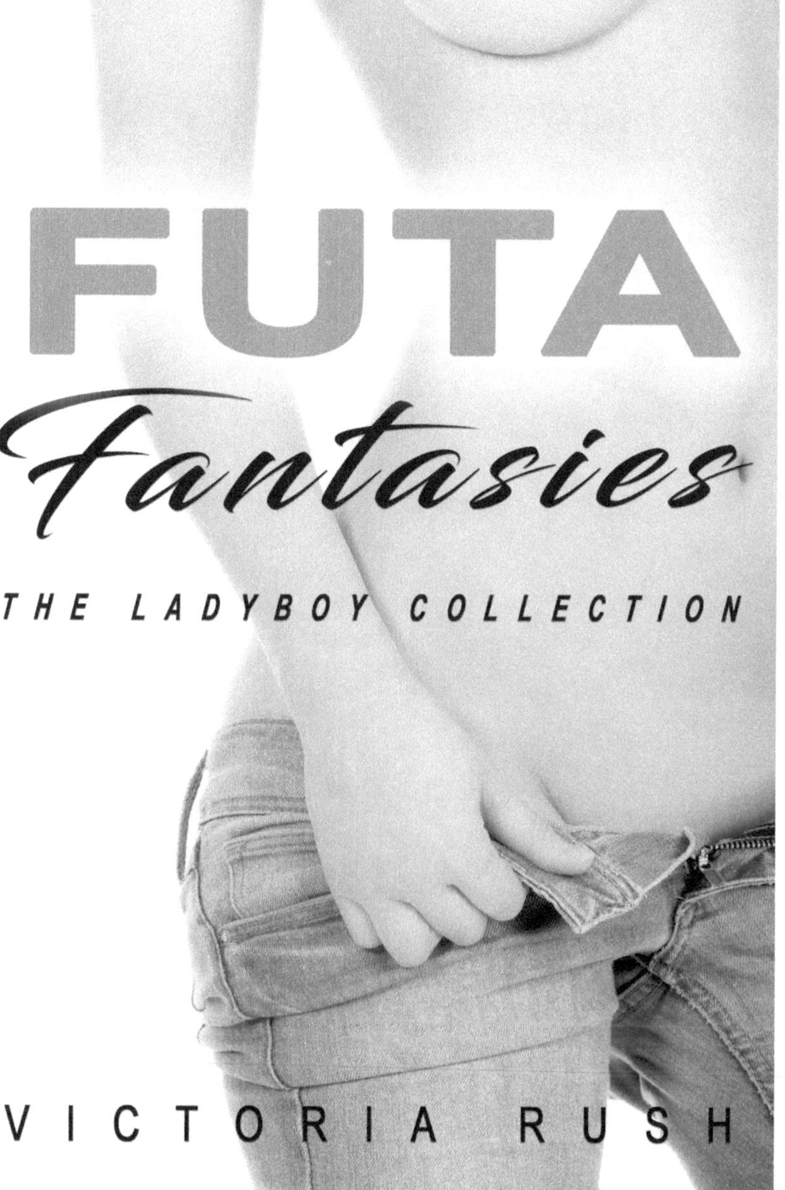

VICTORIA RUSH

Some girls have a little more to work with than others...

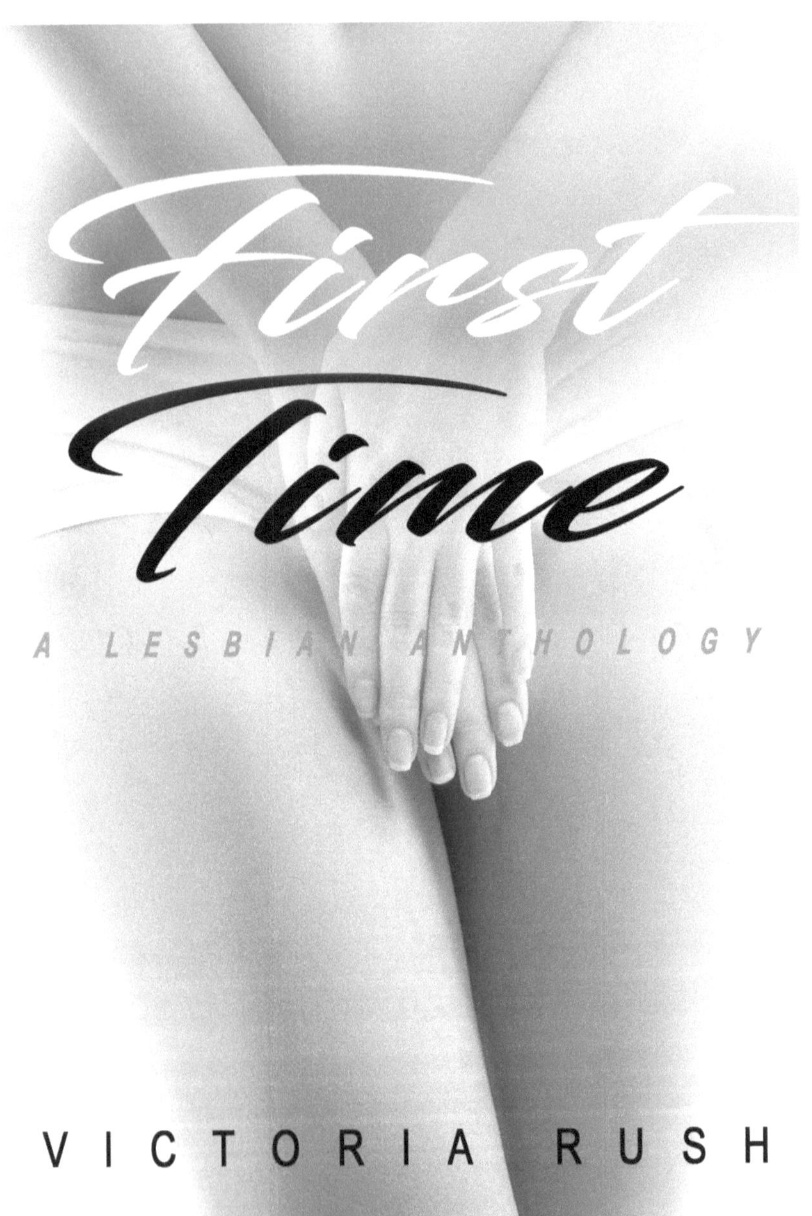

It's never as good as the first time...

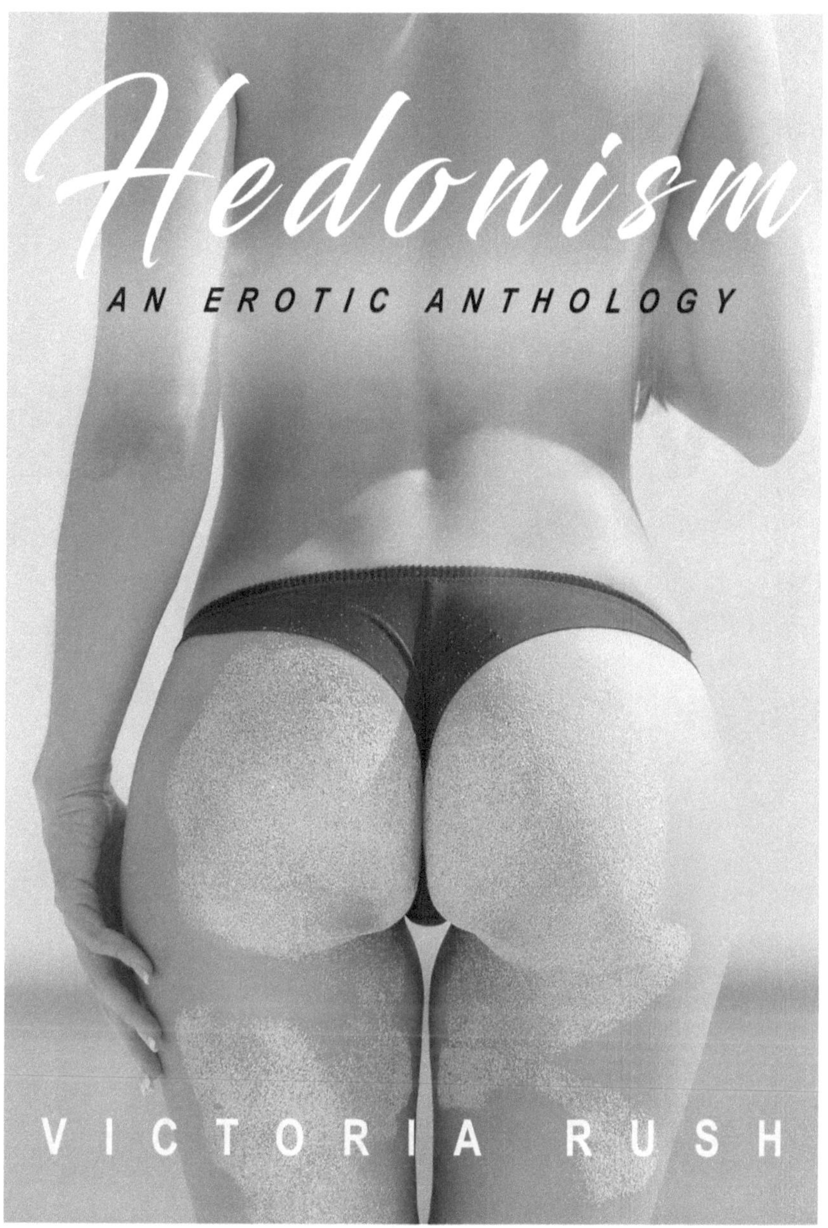

Sometimes all you need to spark up your love life is a little change of scenery...

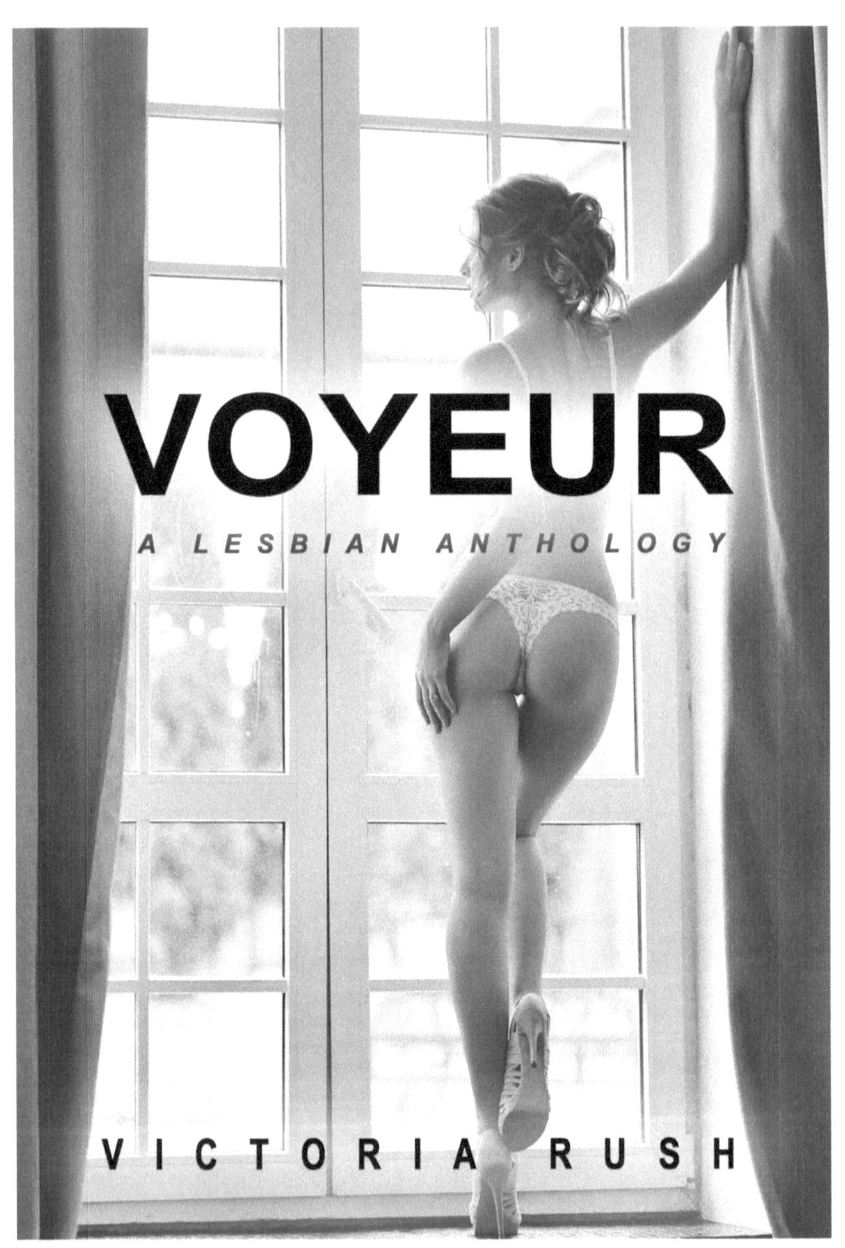

Sometimes it's more fun to watch...